Manu Nellutla

JANYA

BHARATA

The War

This is a work of fiction based on the events mentioned in the epic Mahabharata. Any resemblance to actual persons, living or dead, events, or locales is entirely coincidental.

Book Cover Art by Anjana Chepur
All other images are used under Creative Commons licenses.

ISBN 9798430439217 (Paperback)
ISBN 9798433361928 (Hardcover)
Independently Published

Acknowledgements

I would like to thank my wife Hetal, sons Aarnav and Vihaan for their support and encouragement. It was during one of our dinners that I shared the idea with them and they encouraged me ever since to come up with this book.

Thanks to my parents Raghurama Rao and Indrani, along with my sister Shravya for being my initial readers helping me to refine this book.

Special thanks to the young and talented Anjana Chepur for coming up with the wonderful drawing for the book cover depicting the theme of the book.

Thanks to the many authors, podcasters, writers, and youtubers from whose work I got inspired and got information which helped me in writing this book.

Thanks to the Indian culture which kept the scripture, Mahabharata, as an important tradition over the millennia, which is the reason I started writing this book.

A special thanks to all my relatives and friends who have embraced this book as theirs and continuously encourage me to write.

Remembering my uncle Rasika, and my grandparents Narasimha Rao and Saraswati, with whom I used to watch Mahabharata television series in my childhood. I dedicate this book to them.

Table of Content

Preface _____ 1

Prologue _____ 4

1.Vatsanikaanth Parva _____ 7

2.Sanhanan Parva_____ 22

3.Ishukruth Parva _____ 41

4.Smriti Parva _____ 71

5.Samudyama Parva_____ 88

6.Purva Yuddha Parva _____ 114

7.Yuddha Parva _____ 139

8.Vajraghaata Parva _____ 175

9.Aavrutti Parva_____ 202

10.Bhaisajya Parva _____ 226

End Note _____ 265

Glossary of Terms _____ 266

Preface

It is often questioned whether the events of Mahabharata epic happened or if it was just a fictional. With almost a billion faithful followers of Hinduism (Sanatana Dharma), I am in no position to question one of the most important scriptures of that religion. As a genuine believer and follower of Sanatana Dharma, I believe that Mahabharata events have happened.

Various dates have been suggested as to when the events of Mahabharata might have occurred, ranging from 7000 BCE to 3000 BCE. One thing though that every believer agrees to is that the Mahabharata epic was written depicting the lives of the Kuru clan, especially the cousins Pandavas and Kauravas, their alliances around the Bharata varsha (the current Indian subcontinent), including the famous Sri Krishna who is believed to be an incarnation of God Vishnu, and the epic Kurukshetra war.

As a reader of Mahabharata, I was always captivated by the details in which the scenes, events, discussions and philosophies were written and the depths to which Veda Vyasa, and other later authors who had their own editions have presented the various aspects of the personalities, culture, history, diplomacy, and the battles of those times.

One thing that always intrigued me was that the Mahabharata epic concentrates mostly on the royalty and their feuds. What enticed me into writing this book was the thought of what the common population was going through during those times of epic battles and how were they affected by this war.

Taking the current era into context, we have had many autobiographies or stories of ordinary people and women going through their life struggles during World Wars, from both the Allies and the Axis These were stories not just about the leaders of these nations fighting against each other.

This notion excited me to learn and research more about the lives and culture of the common population during Mahabharata times. Throughout my search, I couldn't find much information. But I didn't want my question and whatever research I have done to go wasted. Hence, my attempt at Janya Bharata, a two-book series, following a tribe based in south-central India during the events around the Kurukshetra war.

In this book, you will see the chapters are titled Parva, similar to the way chapters were called in the Mahabharata epic. You will also note that most of the Kurukshetra war details are accurate based on the information provided in Mahabharata. Most of the names of the kingdoms, kings, army formations, and unfolding events at the

Kurukshetra war have been kept as close to the original information provided in the Mahabharata. A few liberties were taken to add to the fictional pace of the story.

I want to bring to your attention that there are scenes in this book depicting violence especially around battles and sword fighting. Please use your discretion if this book is read by children.

I have provided footnotes for the Sanskrit words which were used in the book, while a glossary of terms is provided at the end of the book for quick reference. The meanings for these words were as closest as I could find since some of the words have multiple meanings. For example, the word Janya itself has many meanings: common, commoner, war and companion.

I hope this book excites you to read further about Mahabharata epic – the greatest scripture ever written.

Manu Nellutla

Prologue

The seeds of animosity between the Pandavas and the Kauravas, the troubled cousins may have been sowed already when Pandu, father of the Pandavas, was crowned as King of Hastinapur instead of his elder brother, Dhritarastra, father of the Kauravas.

Dhritarastra, who was supposed to be the king as per the rules, was not coronated because he was born blind. With the patriarch Bhishma's approval, the younger Pandu was crowned as the king.

But when King Pandu abdicated his throne to pay penance to overcome a curse he was given, there was no other choice for him but to give the reign to his elder brother Dhritarastra. Over time, both the brothers were blessed with sons. Dhritarastra with a hundred of them and Pandu with five.

When Pandu passed away, his wife Kunti along with the five sons stayed at the palace of King Dhritarastra. Though the king was benevolent towards his brother's sons, he always longed that his own son, Duryodhana should take up the reigns instead of Yudhishthira, the eldest son of Pandu, who was also older than Duryodhana.

At the time of recognition of a Crown Prince for the kingdom, Dhritarastra ensured that Duryodhana got that role. Politics ensued which also resulted in the Pandavas sent into exile. When the Pandavas returned from their exile they asked to be provided with at least five villages as Duryodhana was unwilling to make them equal rulers of Hastinapur. Duryodhana refused to that proposition raising the possibility of a war between the cousins.

This led to a diplomatic effort from across the regions, due to the relationships and alliances, to clobber a peace deal between the cousins. Everyone tried their best to pacify Duryodhana but he was one never to budge due to his long-lasting envy of the Pandavas' popularity.

Their cousin, Krishna of Dwarka tried to intervene, along with other patriarchs like Bhishma, Kripacharya and Dronacharya, but to no avail. It has come to the point where a full-blown war between the Pandavas and Kauravas and their respective allies was inevitable.

Map Indian Subcontinent during Mahabharata times.

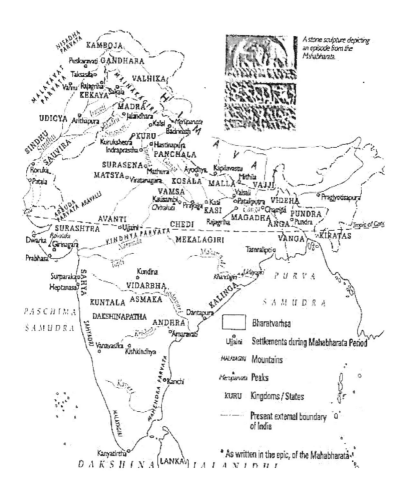

A stone sculpture depicting an episode from the Mahabharata.

☐	Bharatvarhsa
Ujjaini	Settlements during Mahabharata Period
MALAYAGIRI	Mountains
Meruparvata	Peaks
KURU	Kingdoms / States
-----	Present external boundary of India
*	As written in the epic, of the Mahabharata

1.Vatsanikaanth[1] Parva[2]

Purna sat on the steps in front of her home, looking down at the rangavalli[3] her mother had made in the front yard. It was so colorful. *How does my mother come up with these wonderful designs?* she thought. Purna could see the envy in the eyes of women passing by on the street as they looked at this design. Her mother was famous for coming up with unique designs.

As she continued to gaze at the rangavalli, Purna's thoughts meandered, just like the lines of the design. It had been a fortnight since her father and most of the men from Devasthana and nearby

---

[1] Affection towards offspring

[2] Episode/Chapter

[3] Rangoli. Patterns made from powdered limestone.

villages left for the training camp just north of the Vindhya mountain range. She was surprised when her father told her about the call to attend the training camp. He mentioned that all non-disabled men above the age of sixteen, from all the allied tribes of the kingdoms of Kalinga, Pulinda and Andhra regions, were called upon by King Karna of the Anga kingdom to be on standby in case the peace deal between the clashing Kuru princes didn't come to fruition.

This training camp was to prepare for that war, which he hoped would never happen, but her father promised he would return soon. She thought he would be gone for just a few days, but a fortnight seemed long.

She used to get her daily dose of news from around the Bharata varsha[4] through her father, but ever since he went to the camp, she hadn't kept up on the disagreements that were boiling up between the royal Kuru cousins, the Pandavas and the Kauravas. The cousins had been at loggerheads for some years now, and their tussle had kept everyone from across the Himalayas to the Sindhu saagara[5] under tenterhooks.

Purna had so many questions for her father before he left. 'Why can't the cousins fight amongst themselves or come to an agreement?' she asked him. 'Why should they take part in the war, even if it happens?' she would question him. He patiently explained how intricate the relationships between the royals across Bharata

---

[4] Indian subcontinent/land

[5] Ocean/Sea (referring to Indian ocean here)

varsha have been. If one kingdom or clan was at war, the whole subcontinent would be pulled into that war. Most of the royals were either related or had allegiances to each other.

No matter what, it's my father who had to go, Purna thought as she took a deep breath. She moved her gaze away from the rangavalli and looked up at the corner of the street in front of her house. Still no sign of her father. Her friends, Bhumi and Suvarna, had been optimistic that the men may come back from the training camp any day now, as they had heard other elders speaking about the same.

I wish, she thought as she got up to go towards the end of the street to check if her father was at the village gates. There wasn't anyone yet. Purna was getting emotional and angry at the thought of the possibility of her father going to the war.

She had been close to her father since childhood. He was always protective of her, and even more so since she turned fourteen. It's tradition that parents of girls of her age would start searching for a suitable bridegroom for their daughters. Most of the girls got married around her age or before turning seventeen. Bhumi's parents were planning to go to Ramapura village to scout for grooms for her, but the call to attend the training camp changed their plans.

'I don't want to get married,' Purna would say to her father whenever the topic would come up at their home. 'I don't want to leave you both and go away like how mother came here with you,' she would argue. She couldn't digest the fact that she would have to go away from her parents, especially her doting father. Purna always appreciated the extra affection her father showered on her. She loved her mother, but father was different. Mother would ask her to do all the house chores, but her father would always take her out to explore the nearby forest and show her the river in whose name she was named.

Not seeing anyone yet on the road, Purna went back to sit on the steps of her house. The cows, tied to the front yard's fence, were busy grazing the hay while swatting the flies away with their tails. Purna noticed how the red tilakam[6] on the cow's forehead was fading out. Let me put on a fresh coat for them, she thought. Pitashri[7] will be happy to see that. Her father always emphasized how cows and oxen were the most important animals. Being domesticated animals, cows provided dairy products like milk and butter, while the oxen would help in plowing the fields.

She immediately went inside the house to get the vermillion. On the way to the pooja[8] altar, Purna peeked towards the kitchen. She saw her mother was busy cooking. *She must be preparing pitashri's favorite food,* Purna thought. 'Oh Lord Shiva, please let pitashri come home today. Amma[9] has been preparing father's favorite dishes for the past two days in anticipation that he may arrive any day. Please bless us with this wish,' Purna prayed quietly in her mind. She took the small bowl of vermillion kept at the pooja altar and came out of the house.

---

[6] Mark made on forehead with vermillion or sandalwood

[7] Father/Dad

[8] Prayer

[9] Mother/Mom

'Why are you sitting at the door the whole day? Why don't you come and help me here in arranging the plates,' Purna heard her mother as she was coming out of the house.

'I will be back in a minute. I am going to put tilakam on Gowri and Tulasi's forehead,' Purna replied, referring to the names of the two cows. She ran out of the house even before her mother could say anything else.

'Here you go,' Purna said as she rubbed the vermillion on the foreheads of the two cows. 'Pitashri will be happy to see you both too.' She looked towards the street again and saw a few girls rushing towards the corner of the street.

Did the men arrive? she wondered as she went into the house to put the vermillion bowl back at the altar.

'Amma, I will go and check on the main road to see if pitashri and the others have arrived,' Purna informed her mother as she put the bowl back. She ran out as fast as she could. 'Slow down, or you will trip!' her mother shouted. Purna was in no mood to wait.

*****

Mitrajit was tired of walking at this pace for the past one and half days. The vigorous training that they had to participate in at the camp had already tired his body. The canopy of trees was the only solace from the afternoon sun and the heat. He could hear the magpies chirping away in the forest, *possibly communicating to each other about the men walking below on the ground*, he thought.

Mitrajit looked to his left and saw his friend Chitraangad taking a bite from a guava while talking to the chieftain Aparajit. *One more ghadiya[10] and we will reach Devasthana,* Mitrajit thought. He was hungry but didn't want to eat the fruits they packed in the morning. With them being so close to home, it was worth it to wait and eat what his wife Dhruti must have cooked. He missed eating home cooked food all these days. The food at the camp was good enough, but not as spicy as he wanted it to be. He always felt that Dhruti cooked the best spicy food.

All the while, coming back from the training camp, he couldn't stop thinking of the possibility of this war. He could understand that the training was to ensure that everyone was prepared for the war, but how mentally prepared were each one of them for that possibility? Not a bit, he reckoned. Most of them were there because of the alliances or an eagerness to show off their skills.

The one thing he was most worried was the unsureness of the outcome of a potential war. Would he come back safely to his family? If something happened to him, how would his family take that news? Mitrajit kept thinking about all the questions he must be prepared for in case of an undesirable outcome.

As he paced himself in the forest, he made sure he crossed the huge roots of the trees that were popping out of the ground. *So many obstacles when the destination is so near*, he thought. Of course, he was not new to challenges. Whether it was a childhood made up of the

---

[10] Unit of Time – one ghadiya equals approximately 24 minutes

attacks of the dreaded Ekapaadas, the time when his father died, or the time he and his wife, Dhruti, had to endure the doubts and questions from some of the villagers about not having kids sooner. *At the end of every tunnel, there has been light,* he thought as he was nearing the edge of the forest area.

He reminisced how he and Dhruti had to pass through the same forest area to make a special trip to the riverbanks of the maata[11] Godavari. Once there, to be blessed with a child, they prayed for three nights and days at the jyotirlinga[12] without eating food or drinking water. The prayers did work for them, as later that year they were blessed with a girl child. Mitrajit's eyes swelled with the praise he had for Dhruti for standing up to all that flak she used to receive from some villagers. *She truly justifies the meaning of her name,* he thought. The child made their life content and hence was named Purna, meaning complete, which was also the name of a tributary of Godavari river.

Mitrajit could now see the brown fence walling that surrounded Devasthana. The bushes and thorny branches that they put around the village as a protection from any attackers and wild animals from the forest had started drying up. They needed to be checked again to ensure the branches were strong enough to endure the next few months. He looked up towards the village and saw the smoke from the houses. *Prepping up for lunch probably*, he thought.

---

[11] Mother – used here in context of respecting the river Godavari
[12] Special shrine where Lord Shiva is worshiped

*****

Devasthana, along with the surrounding twelve villages, made up the region in the central Bharata varsha and around the Godavari river's tributary Purna. It was this region that the Ustrakarnika tribe called home. Over the past many centuries this region had been independent, though in close alliance with the Kalinga kingdom in the east.

The Ustrakarnikas were famous for their swordsmanship. Though they were focused on the military training irrespective of gender, every Ustrakarnika was also encouraged to know other trades including farming and business. This was to ensure there was no discrimination within the tribe based on their work. It also allowed them to be self-reliant.

The geographical location played an important role in allowing them to be independent; its blocked off nature made it difficult for any attackers to reach Devasthana and nearby villages. The Purna tributary served as a barrier on the eastern side while the thick old growth trees and wild animals in the forest both on the north and west of the region helped as a deterrent. It was only in the south that they didn't have any natural defenses, which they buttressed further by fences and digging up the trenches which extended to both the western and eastern sides of the village.

The defenses were needed to keep away the attacks from their archrivals, the Ekapaadas, the tribe from the south. The rivalry between Ekapaada and Ustrakarnika tribes was centuries old. The

Ustrakarnikas were peace seeking and had a non-proliferation approach, but not the Ekapaadas. Ustrakarnikas had to, over the past few generations, deal with regular attacks from the Ekapaada tribes. Though the Ustrakarnikas were able to thwart most of these guerilla type attacks, they were concerned about the continuous efforts and resources required to keep them at bay.

This led the Ustrakarnikas to approach the Kalingas on the east for an alliance. The Kalingas were happy to support the Ustrakarnikas due to the long-standing trade agreements they already had. The Kalingas promised to support them with troops if a large-scale war happened between the tribes. As part of this diplomatic alliance with the Kalinga kingdom, Ustrakarnikas had to regularly pay taxes to the Kalinga treasury. Since the alliance was announced the attacks by the Ekapaadas reduced, thus allowing a peaceful few years for the Ustrakarnikas.

The only time Devasthana came close to being attacked in recent times was when Yudhishthira, the elder of the Pandavas, was crowned the king of Indraprastha. As part of the Rajasuya Yagna[13], he sent his brothers including Sahadeva across the Bharata varsha to confirm his sovereignty over the area. The tribal regions and kingdoms across the lands had to either agree and send gifts or refuse and be seen as opposing the king. This once in a generation ritual put Devasthana and Ustrakarnikas close to being attacked by Sahadeva's army.

---

[13] Imperial sacrifice or royal inauguration sacrifice/consecration of king

Thanks to their alliance with the Kalinga kingdom, who in turn were closer to king Karna of the Anga kingdom in the north east, the Ustrakarnika's chieftain Aparajit used his diplomacy to ensure that Sahadeva didn't attack their region. It also helped that King Karna was a close friend of king Duryodhana, the eldest of the Kauravas. Pandavas would not have wanted to fight with Kauravas at that point.

Though, when the news spread around the lands that the dispute between Pandavas and Kauravas on who should be ruling the Kuru clan wasn't ending and that they were in their final attempts at peace, the Ustrakarnikas got concerned. Their worries were confirmed when they received notification from the Kalinga kingdom to gather at the training camp, north of the Vindhya Mountains, to prepare for a war in case the peace negotiations failed between the royal cousins. It was also an attempt to send a message to the Pandavas of how the Kauravas along with their allies were well prepared in case the Pandavas wanted to fight.

*****

Mitrajit saw kids from Devasthana running towards them as they started entering the village gates. The kids were happy to see their fathers and brothers back from the training camp. The commotion led the women and elderly come out of their homes. Everyone looked excited to have their men back home.

16

'Glad to be back. There is something special about this place. Talk to you later.' Chitraangad said as he headed towards his home. Mitrajit nodded to acknowledge his friend's statement and picked up his pace walking towards his house.

Mitrajit saw Purna running in his direction just as he turned towards the corner of the street leading home. He was a bit worried she may fall by tripping on her paridhana[14] at the pace she was running. He was so happy to see her. He immediately put down his sword and shield, kneeled down to reach her, and opened his arms. Purna went straight into her father's arms and hugged him tight. 'I missed you, pitashri,' Purna said. She was happy to feel the warm embrace and strong arms of her father again. She always felt protected with him beside her.

Looking at her daughter's face and innocent hazel eyes, for a moment Mitrajit forgot about the tiredness and hard-working days over the past weeks at the training camp.

He was home. He was happy to get a break from the camp to come and see his family. He was feeling good about being told that he was missed. At that moment, he wanted to forget all the anxiety he was going through on his way back about how to explain to his daughter the possibilities of him going to war. *Let me not think about that now,* he thought as he continued to hug his daughter. *Today is a day of spending time with my family, getting all the attention, and showering all my love on them.*

---

[14] Lower garment or clothing

Mitrajit eased his arms a bit, making sure his armor didn't hurt her. 'Purna, my dear, I missed you too. First tell me about what all you have been up to these past few weeks. Hope you were good to your mother?' He had to ask that question.

'Surprisingly, your daughter has been on her best behavior this time. But now that you are here, we will have to see how spoiled she will be now with your pampering,' quipped Dhruti while coming towards them.

Mitrajit looked up to see Dhruti wearing a saffron colored saree. Mitrajit smiled as he got up and gave her a hug. He moved her curly hair falling onto her face and planted a kiss on her forehead. Dhruti's cheeks turned red in embarrassment as she didn't expect him to express his affection in public.

'See, even amma agrees,' Purna replied, bringing Mitrajit and Dhruti to her attention. 'I was on my best behavior. pitashri. Now come quickly with me, I want to show you something.' Purna held her father's hand and pulled him towards their house.

'Let your father freshen up and eat something. He must be tired from the journey,' Dhruti insisted. But Purna was in no mood to listen. She continued pulling Mitrajit towards the house. Mitrajit looked at Dhruti and smiled, knowing she would understand the eagerness of their child at seeing him after many days.

'I will keep the plantain fry ready for you. Come and eat when your daughter allows you to', she said with a teasing tone, knowing that the mention of his favorite dish may make him want to come home sooner.

Mitrajit raised his eyebrows in surprise as he gave a smile and went with Purna towards the gate.

The fence on this side needs to be fixed, he thought as he was passing by the side of the house. After crossing the well and the backyard, they reached the farmland. Mitrajit inherited this small piece of farmland and had been growing various seasonal vegetables here. The farm along with the barn took most of the space behind his home till the edge of the hillock on the eastern side.

Purna took Mitrajit closer to the barn towards the Peepal[15] tree which had been there since his childhood; he himself had many memories playing around it. 'There he is.' she said, pointing to the base of the tree. At first, Mitrajit couldn't see anything. But then, he saw it: camouflaged with the tree's base was a small squirrel. Mitrajit looked curiously at Purna.

Purna quickly bent down and picked up the squirrel in her palm. 'Look.' She was delighted to show it to her father.

Mitrajit was surprised and still curious to see that the rodent didn't run away. 'How are you able to hold a wild squirrel? It is not that easy to do so.'

'Oh, he is not wild. He is so gentle. When you were at the training camp, I used to come to spend time under the tree's shade in the afternoons. I started observing that Moksha was living on this tree. He would come down daily to collect food and one day I offered him a guava fruit that I was having, and he took it.'

---

[15] A species of fig tree

19

Mitrajit interrupted her, 'Wait a minute. You named it Moksha!'

'Oh yes. I gave that name based on the story you told me about *prabhu*[16] Ram. Remember? You mentioned that a little squirrel attained *moksha*[17] because he was blessed by prabhu Ram for helping his own little way in building the Nala-Nila *Sethu*[18] when prabhu Ram and his army wanted to cross the ocean to reach Lanka.'

Those words made Mitrajit's eyes swell with tears of happiness. 'I like that name, good choice,' he said. He was so amazed by his daughter. Not only was she wise and intelligent, but she was also so passionate. *Thank you, Lord Shiva, for blessing us with this daughter,* he prayed as he put his hand on his heart. 'Now, let's go before your mother gets angry with us for being late,' he said.

'Last one to reach the house will get to clean the pooja altar,' Purna said as she dashed home.

---

[16] Sir/Lord – mark of respect

[17] Emancipation/liberation

[18] Bridge

2.Sanhanan[19] Parva

Dhruti was waiting impatiently at home for the father-daughter duo to come for lunch. She was so happy to see Mitrajit. It was not very often that he had to go away for such long duration. Most of the visits had been a day or two at the maximum, such as when he would accompany chieftain Aparajit to visit other villages or Kalinga kingdom.

Now that Mitrajit was back from the camp, she was eager to spend time with him. It was not easy for the women in Devasthana while the men were away at the training camp. They were stressed at the thought of the outcome of the Kuru family feud. They were

---

[19] Patience/hardening of soul

concerned that if the war was inevitable then their husbands, sons, brothers would have to go and participate.

Why do common people like us have to be brought into this dispute between families? Do the Pandavas and Kauravas understand the consequences of entering this war? What are all the wise men around them doing? Can't they help in negotiations? May be Mitrajit knows the latest updates, Dhruti thought as she arranged the plates for lunch.

She went to the back door to check on them. She saw Purna showing the squirrel to Mitrajit. *How excited our little girl is to have her father back from the camp,* she thought. But how would she take it if he had to go back to the camp again? How would they tell her? How would any father tell his kid that he has to go to a war and there could be many chances that he might not return? Dhruti's mind wandered all over these questions until she was brought back to reality by Purna passing by her hurriedly to get into the house. She looked out to see Mitrajit getting close to the back door. His body was shining from the tiny amounts of sweat reflecting the afternoon sun. *His body looked in better shape than before due to the training at the camp,* she thought.

Mitrajit looked at Dhruti as he was coming towards the house. He could sense that Dhruti was lost in her thoughts. He looked at her and gave a smile. He was about to talk to her when Purna came out and said, 'Amma, I am hungry,'

'Yes, me too!' Mitrajit responded. He didn't want Dhruti to be bogged down by worries now. All the uncertainties could wait. For now, all Mitrajit wanted was to spend time with his family.

'Sure. Why don't you freshen up and come? If not for your daughter's eagerness to show you the squirrel, we would be eating by now,' Dhruti replied. Mitrajit laughed at that response. He enjoyed whenever Dhruti felt that he showered more of his affection towards Purna. I came into your life first, she would always say in her defense.

Mitrajit went towards the well to take a bath. As he poured the cold water on his body, he felt a sense of freshness and rejuvenation after that long trip from the camp. Once ready, he came into the kitchen to see Dhruti had arranged the dishes on the floor. Purna tapped on the ground to show where she wanted him to sit, right beside her.

Sitting on the bhitti[20] that Dhruti herself had woven, Mitrajit was happy to see that she really had prepared his favorite plantain fry dish. Plantains were the easiest to find near the riverbank and it was the dish his mother used to cook for him too.

Purna was excited to sit beside her father and have lunch after so many days. Lunch and dinner were the times of the day when the three of them would sit together, eat, talk, and share stories. Father would tell events from his childhood and how he had grown up, how and when he met mother, and update her with all the news across the land.

---

[20] Woven mat

'So how was it at the training camp? What is going on with the Kuru cousins? Are they going to fight a war? Do you need to go back?' Purna kept on asking questions.

'Can you not wait till he's had his lunch?' Dhruti replied. She wanted to make sure Mitrajit enjoyed his meal after many days of hard work.

'It is okay, Dhruti. Let her ask. She is curious to know,' Mitrajit said. Looking at Purna, he said, 'The training camp was interesting as we learnt different war strategies and rules. We had lot of time to practice some of the routines and tactics. Though we all hope that we don't have to use any of them. But the rules were interesting. Do you know that one of the rules is to fight only between sunrise and sunset? So, no more sneak attacks like the Ekapaadas would bring upon us.'

'Oh, that's interesting. Acharya[21] ji[22] was mentioning in one of his classes that the elder Kuru royal Bhishma is a very ethical warrior, and he will ensure that if a war happens, it would be according to some rules,' Purna replied eagerly to impress her father.

'Good to know that you learnt about that Purna. Your acharya is wise enough to tell you that.' Mitrajit replied.

'Can we not discuss the training and wars right now and talk about the dish I prepared for you?' Dhruti intervened to change the topic.

---

[21] Teacher

[22] A mark of respect. Like Sir/Madam.

'I don't taste anything different.' Purna was quick to give her opinion. Mitrajit looked at Dhruti for her reaction to that statement.

'See. I told you. Now that you are back, she is onto her usual behavior,' Dhruti complained to him.

'Ha-ha. Okay. Let's finish this amazing lunch and then I would like to take some rest. Looks like my body needs it after those long days at the camp and the journey back. I would love to get some sleep.' Mitrajit said.

'Of course, pitashri. But promise to tell me more at dinner time. I am eager to hear about the tactics you learnt. Maybe you can teach me some,' Purna replied.

'Definitely, dear,' Mitrajit said as he got up to wash his hands.

*****

After lunch, Purna went to play with her friends. All the kids were excited to share their happiness of meeting their family members after two weeks. For some it was their fathers and for some it was their brothers. Elders in Devasthana were happy to see the bustle at the chatvaram[23] of the village where all the kids gathered and played.

Mitrajit stretched his body and laid down on the bed. The mattress below made it comfortable for him, unlike at the camp where he had to sleep on a makeshift bed. His eyes started getting heavier and within minutes he was fast asleep.

---

[23] Four corners/crossroads/main center

'I feel so refreshed,' Mitrajit said as he came into the living room after taking an afternoon nap for almost three ghadiyas. He looked around and saw Dhruti sitting alone on the steps in the backyard. She looked deep in her thoughts.

'Ah, here you are,' Mitrajit said as he approached her. He sat beside and looked at her. Her eyes were turning red from the various thoughts she has been having.

'I hope you understand, Dhruti,' he said, looking deep into her eyes. 'This is not just about our tribe and the village but also for the future of Purna,' he continued. 'We would want her to grow up in a peaceful land, no matter which family she gets married into.'

'You don't need to explain further to me, swami[24],' Dhruti replied looking into Mitrajit's concerned eyes. 'We have all been preparing for this for the past few weeks. Summoning you for the training camp itself was a hint that this is going to lead to something bigger. When powerful dynasties are at odds to come to an agreement it is understandable that we commoners will be affected. What else can we do?'

She looked down towards the floor, not wanting him see her tear-filled eyes. 'My only worry is what if something happens to you? How are we going to survive? How are we going to get Purna married? We don't have any other close family left.'

Mitrajit's heart was pounding hard listening to her voice. Dhruti always portrayed herself as a strong lady but at the core, she was still

---

[24] Husband/mark of respect

the beautiful, soft-spoken woman that he got married to decades ago. Thinking about Purna's future made him feel sadder. Dhruti was right. *What if the war did go ahead and he didn't come back?* He should have thought about finding a suitable man for Purna earlier. He always felt she was too young to be married and thought of postponing the search for the bridegroom for a few more years.

He lifted Dhruti's face with his hand under her chin. Her tears started rolling down from her eyes. Wiping off the tears from her face, Mitrajit said, 'Well, for now let us hope there is not going to be any war. And even if it is going ahead, let us wish that we will be safe and back. At the same time, we need to be prepared for the worst. If I must go, I better go prepared. I will finish off the maintenance repairs for our barn so that it doesn't trouble you when I am gone. I know we have saved enough grain for the next two seasons in the barn, but if something worse happens to me or our tribe, we know that the Kalinga kingdom has promised to send in supplies as part of our alliance.'

Dhruti nodded in agreement. She had to be strong. She wiped off the tears and took a deep breath. 'I am sorry, swami. Though I have been preparing mentally for this, I still got worried. But let us hope that the peace negotiations are successful.'

'Of course, my dear. Let us hope so. But I think we have to talk to Purna and have her be prepared for the worst. I hope she will understand,' Mitrajit said.

'Don't worry about her, swami. I have been hinting to Purna that you may be asked to go back again should there be a war. She is our clever girl. She will understand. If the war happens, all I ask maata Godavari is for your safe return and to get Purna married.' Dhruti joined both her hands as in a prayer.

'I promise that if there is a war then I will get back home safely,' Mitrajit replied with assurance. Especially as it was close to dusk, he didn't want to think negatively. When he was young, his parents told him about the thathaastu[25] devatas[26] or Ashwini devatas. It seems these devatas would make anything you mentioned out loud during the dusk into a reality. Since then, he believed it diligently. All he wanted today was for these thathaastu devatas to listen to his positive thoughts.

Just then, Purna came running in and announced, 'Pitashri, do you have to go back to the training camp by Thursday.' They both were shocked to hear what Purna had to say. So, the last minute try at the peace deal by Krishna must not have worked and they had only three more days to go back.

'Where did you hear about that Purna?' Mitrajit inquired while kneeling to reach her at eye level.

'I heard at the chatvaram. It seems Aparajit ji has summoned the villagers to meet there in the next ghadiya,' she said with a worried look on her face.

Looking at his kid, he realized it was better to mention it now than to wait. 'Look, dear, remember I told you before going to the

---

[25] Blessing/outcomes

[26] Gods

camp that this could lead to a long war, and as you heard, it turns out that they are going into a war. You know we must honor our alliance with the Kalinga kingdom. So, we must go. But don't worry, your mother is going to take care of you, and I will be back home in no time.' He tried to put on a brave face during the last sentence.

'I understand, pitashri. Do not worry about me and mother. I will be on my best behavior and support her as I have been in the past few weeks. I have been learning to cook and have been cleaning our barn too. I am a big girl now. All I wish is for you to come back safely' Purna replied.

It must have been my past life's good deeds that I was blessed with such an understanding wife and wise child, Mitrajit thought. 'Of course, dear. Now come here and give me a hug. The next two days you are going to help me in fixing the barn and the fences.' he replied.

Two men at the door knocked to get the family's attention. 'Excuse us for our interference, Mitrajit ji. The chieftain wanted everyone to gather at the chatvaram within the next ghadiya. He has some announcements to make and wanted to see you before that.'

'Sure. Thank you for the information. I will start soon.' Mitrajit replied. He saw the two men leave the main door and go towards the next house. Turning to Dhruti and Purna, he said, 'I will be leaving. I need to connect with Aparajit before everyone reaches. You may want to join there with others.'

30

Before leaving the house, Mitrajit went towards the pooja altar. He bowed down and sought blessings from the linga[27] that was placed at the altar. 'Oh, Lord Shiva, please bless us to be safe and return home safely,' Mitrajit prayed quietly.

*****

By the time Mitrajit arrived at the chatvaram, he saw Chitraangad sitting on the platform beside Aparajit and talking to him. Aparajit looked at Mitrajit and said, 'Come sit here, Mitra. We got news from the Kalingas that the peace deal was not fruitful and that the Pandavas and Kauravas have declared war against each other. We must leave in three days so that we can arrive at the training camp before heading further north to Kurukshetra, the designated battlefield. It is time to announce this to the rest of the villagers.'

Mitrajit nodded to acknowledge the news. *There is nothing much anyone can do now,* he thought. The only positive thing was that they were able to get back from the camp to spend some time with the families before heading back for an unknown future.

As the crowd started gathering, Aparajit stood up along with Mitrajit and Chitraangad and held his hand high to calm down the commotion.

---

[27] Idol for worshipping Lord Shiva

'Namaskaram[28] everyone. You all must be eager to know why I have gathered you all at such short notice. We left the training camp few days ago with the anticipation of some news regarding the ongoing efforts to strike a peace deal between the Pandavas and the Kauravas. We received a note today from King Srutayush of the Kalinga kingdom that Duryodhana and the Kauravas disagreed with Krishna for any peaceful negotiations with the powerful Pandavas. He was not even ready to give the five villages that Krishna proposed to give to the five brothers. With the failure of the peace negotiations, Pandavas have announced war on the Kauravas. King Karna of the Anga kingdom has called on all his allies to join him in his support for the Kauravas. Kurukshetra in the north has been selected as the battle zone. We must leave in three days from now so that we can reach the training camp where we will be joined by our allies Kalinga and Anga kingdom's forces.' Aparajit took a brief pause to gauge the response from the crowd. They all appeared to be in shock at the news.

'I understand this is not what you wanted to hear. This is also definitely not what I wanted to hear too, though we all were preparing for this moment in case of the peace deal not moving forward.' His voice became heavier as he mentioned that.

---

[28] Greetings

'I have discussed with acharya ji, and he has suggested that we conduct a yagna[29] in two days at the midday muhurat[30] to pray for the success of our participation and continued prosperity for our tribe. He will make the necessary arrangements and we will all meet at the temple. I have asked Chitraangad to let the other villages be aware of the news and invite them to join us for the yagna.'

'The next three days are important for us to also spend time with our loved ones,' Aparajit continued. 'I also want to reassure to the elders and women that we will review our defenses to make sure the women, kids and elders will be safe. I will update if there is any other news.'

Aparajit ended the way he always did in his speeches. Clear and affirmative. Even if there was any hesitation or softness in thoughts, Mitrajit found it was never evident in the way he delivered it. He had always been the astute leader that the Ustrakarnikas needed. There was so much Mitrajit had learnt from his leader from all these years.

The crowd took its time to come to the terms and slowly started leaving the chatvaram. Chitraangad went towards his wife Subhadra and said, 'So that was the news. I will have to work with our men to ensure the message is sent to the rest of the villages.'

Subhadra didn't look pleased at the news. *Who would be?* Chitraangad thought. 'Subhadra, you know we have to go.'

---

[29] Special prayer/ceremonial rights to God

[30] Auspicious time of the day

33

'I understand, swami, but I am not yet prepared to have our son go to war. He is just seventeen,' Subhadra replied.

'Amma, don't embarrass me. I am strong and old enough to fight,' Arochan said. Chitraangad looked at his son and smiled. He knew that Arochan was young, but he was at an age when most of the men got enrolled into armies and ready to fight.

'Subhadra, your son has grown up. He is going to fight alongside other mighty warriors. This war will be a great learning experience for him. I will be there all along and ensure our boy is safe.' Chitraangad put his arm around Arochan. *This young boy with these broad shoulders would give anyone a run for their life,* Chitraangad thought.

'And I will also be keeping a close eye on him,' Mitrajit said as he came towards them with Dhruti and Purna.

Subhadra looked at Mitrajit and said, 'You should definitely teach some more of your calmness to these two. Otherwise I know these two are excited to fight.'

'Well, that's what we trained for,' Chitraangad replied. 'But I promise to be cautious and safe,' he continued to say to calm his nervous wife.

Just then, Aparajit, along with his wife Kumudini, came towards Mitrajit and Chitraangad's families. 'I hope we all will sail through this without any troubles. I know and am confident that Devasthana will be in the good hands of Kumudini,' Aparajit said, looking at her.

'With Subhadra and Dhruti and the rest of the elders' support, I feel we can manage till you all can come back,' Kumudini replied while putting her hands together to pray while she mentioned those last words.

There was a moment of silence among the group. They all could sense the anxiousness surrounding them, but at the same time as a group of leaders who were looked up to by others in the tribe, they had to be seen as tough and under control of their emotions.

'Yes, with the grace of Lord Shiva we will come back,' Mitrajit intervened to break the impasse. 'Yes, we will,' Chitraangad followed up in a reassuring tone.

*****

That evening, Mitrajit sat in front of the pooja altar and went into the posture of padmasana[31]. If there was one thing he had not missed doing since his adolescent age was spending at least a ghadiya meditating every day. He learnt it from his mother who emphasized that no matter what troubles you have, a ghadiya of meditation will take it away and calm down one's nerves.

Seeing Mitrajit sit quietly in his meditation pose, Dhruti signaled Purna to come into the backyard. Sitting on the steps of the backyard, she said, 'Purna, dear, you know like with any of the wars, we can never guess the outcome of this one too, but all we can hope and pray for is for the safe return of your pitashri and everyone else in the village. We both need to demonstrate to him that we are

---

[31] Crossed legged sitting

35

comfortable with all that he has provided to us and that we will be safe when he is out there fighting in the war. You are a wise girl and I know you will understand this.'

'Of course, amma. Don't you worry about that. I want to make sure I will not show any worry or express it to pitashri. But at the same time, I am really worried about what will happen to him during the war, amma. I hope and pray that he comes back safely.' Purna gave Dhruti a big hug. Dhruti was moved by that. Poor child, she had to endure such challenges thanks to the scuffle between the princely groups.

'I understand, dear. Don't worry, all will be well. If it wasn't for the mighty soldiers who helped prabhu Ram, he couldn't have easily succeeded on Ravana. It is because of the bravery of warriors like your father that the kings and princes are successful in their campaigns. I just hope that this war doesn't turn out into a big one with troubling outcomes. I hope sense prevails among the fighting Kurus and come to peace.' Dhruti sounded optimistic as she mentioned that.

'So, this is how you both spend your evenings nowadays, sitting on the steps and conversing,' Mitrajit said as he came towards the back door. He was amused to see the mother and daughter together, talking and bonding with each other. It was always him who would engage Purna in a conversation. Dhruti's conversations with Purna had lately been around working on the chores. Dhruti wanted to make sure Purna was prepared for wedded life.

Making sure he didn't hear any of their previous conversation, Dhruti replied, 'Ha-ha. We were discussing about the dishes to be prepared in the next two days so that you can enjoy them.'

'I would love to have Pulasa³² fish for sure,' Mitrajit replied. If he had only a few days to enjoy the food prepared by his wife, it was either Plantain or Pulasa dish.

'I will help in cooking amma. I would love to learn how to cook the fish,' Purna replied.

'Sure, dear. Let's get the fish from the market first thing in the morning. Meanwhile, let me go and prepare for today's dinner. Do you want to give me a hand?' Dhruti said while getting up slowly from the steps. Purna replied with a nod and a shrug. 'What does that mean?' Dhruti asked.

'Well, do I have a choice?!' Purna quipped and ran into the house before Dhruti raised her hand to tap on her shoulder. Mitrajit laughed at Purna's reply.

'I know you may be amused at her reply...' Dhruti complained.

'Okay, okay. It's all my fault. Agreed.' Mitrajit couldn't stop laughing. 'You both sort it out while I will go and connect with Chitraangad.'

'Sure. One more thing,' she said as he turned to leave. 'I was thinking that we should all have dinner together tomorrow. Please do invite them. I know if you mention about the Pulasa dish, Chitra

---

³² Ilis or Hilsha fish

braathaa[33] will be here even before we start preparing to cook. He loves that dish so much.'

'Ha-ha. True. See you later!' Mitrajit replied as he went towards the main door. He wanted to check on his good friend after today's announcement.

Mitrajit opened the main door and was surprised to see Chitraangad walking towards their door in the front yard.

'I wanted to check up on you,' Chitraangad said, looking at his friend coming out of the house. Mitrajit was not surprised to see him. He knew Chitraangad must be eager, like himself, to know if he was keeping up well with the news.

'Same here, Chitra. I was planning to come to your house too. Let us go for a stroll around the neighborhood and talk,' Mitrajit said while signing to his friend that it may be better to discuss outside so that Dhruti and Purna may not hear them.

'So, what do you think? How are you feeling?' Mitrajit asked once they were outside the gates of his house.

'What else to say, Mitra. We knew this may happen so at least we are prepared. I am pumped up to put my sword into action, but I am worried for Subhadra. She is not able to digest the fact that Arochan must go with us for the war. She was already cautious when we went to the camp but now, she looks worrisome. How is Dhruti taking it?'

---

[33] Brother

Mitrajit smiled when Chitraangad mentioned about putting his sword to action. Everyone in the village was aware of this chest-thumping, brave, and aggressive side of him.

'Dhruti is definitely hiding her concerns and putting on a brave face. She thinks I don't recognize that. Well, what can we do? We knew this was coming ever since the Pandavas were sent to exile by Duryodhana. All we could do is go, fight to our best ability, shield ourselves and hope to come back alive without any injuries.' Mitrajit joined his two hands in a gesture of prayer as he finished that sentence.

'Of course, we will come back alive. Our swordsmanship will help us,' Chitraangad said as he twirled his moustache. 'I can't wait to go. Anyways, Aparajit has assigned me the task of going tomorrow morning to communicate across other villages. I will be back probably by late evening. Arochan is helping Subhadra gather things in the barn and hope you can check in with them if they need anything.'

'Sure, Chitra. I will. When you get back from your trip in the evening, come along and join us for dinner with our family. Dhruti is cooking Pulasa.'

'Oh, Pulasa! Why didn't you say it earlier?' Chitraangad replied while smacking his friend's arm. 'I will make sure I am there at your house before sunset.'

Mitrajit chuckled at Chitraangad's reply. 'Make sure you do deliver the message and don't rush back for the dinner,' he replied teasingly.

'Ha-ha. You know me,' Chitraangad said as started going towards him home, waving to his friend.

Mitrajit waved back and headed back home. Two more days with family. Need to make the most of it, he thought.

3.Ishukruth[34] Parva

By morning the villagers gathered for the yagna at the temple premises. Devasthana was decorated well for this occasion with flowers. Everyone felt the need to send the men to the war with high spirits though everyone had a poignant look on their faces.

Acharya took his time to prepare the yagna platform with elaborate details. As per the rules of the book, a shayana chithi[35] was prepared for the yagna emphasizing that the prayer was performed for prosperity of the Ustrakarnika tribe.

---

[34] Preparation

[35] Platform in shape of Eagle/Falcon

Some of the elders in the village requested for a Prauga chithi[36] which emphasized that the prayers were made to destroy the enemies. Aparajit refused that request. He insisted that instead of praying for destruction of their enemy, it was much more ethical to pray for their own prosperity. Not everyone was participating with the motive to fight the Pandavas or the Kauravas. Alliances, relationships, and friendships were the reasons that compelled the others to join this war, Aparajit argued.

As they were getting ready to go to the event, Dhruti saw that Purna didn't look eager to go to the yagna. Purna always enjoyed events and festivities like these. She was interested in Jyotishya[37] as a subject and her acharya always encouraged her to learn about how different forms and shapes in a yagna influenced the astrological realm.

'I know you are struggling with this, dear. Even I am. But you know this yagna is conducted to with the intention to protect your father and all we can do is pray and wish for Lord Shiva to bless us. You don't want your father to go with the thought that we were worried for him. We want him to concentrate on the task ahead and come back safely from the war,' Dhruti said to bolster Purna's morale.

'Yes, amma. I am sorry that I made it obvious from my expression. I will make sure that I put on a smile,' Purna replied while

---

[36] Platform in shape of triangle

[37] Astrology

trying to smile. Dhruti gave her a hug and kissed on her forehead. 'I am proud of you, Purna. Not just me. Me and your pitashri, both are proud of you. Now let's get ready and head out to the temple.'

*****

The past two days had been busy for Mitrajit. He made sure that the barn was repaired and filled with grain needed at least for two more seasons. He also fixed the fence on the side of the house, all the while being optimistic that he would come back. As one of the soldiers from the many Akshauhinis[38] that would be fighting in the war, no one would be concerned if he survived or not. *But it is my family that will suffer*, Mitrajit's thoughts started wandering off as he was checking the fence around the barn.

Did not he have a choice of not participating in the war? Well, he would be ridiculed for not participating. Every abled man was considered an asset for the troops required during the battles. And this was not any normal battle, this is a major war between the two Kuru families. It's a war which will decide who will control not only the capital Hastinapura but also exert their influence across the Bharata varsha. Never has a war raged that had this level of importance on this land.

––––––––––––

[38] A battle formation with an Akshauhini consisting of 21,870 each of chariots and elephants, 65,160 horses and 109,350 of infantry.

Even if he had any concerns or thoughts of not coming back safely, Mitrajit didn't want to show it to Dhruti and Purna. He could sense that they were also hiding their feelings.

After Chitraangad came back from his day trip from other villages to announce the departure dates and the invitation to attend the yagna, he along with Subhadra and Arochan joined Mitrajit and family for dinner. Everyone looked in deep thoughts and in a tense mood during the dinner with the thought that this could be the last time they all were being together.

Chitraangad looked around and to break the tense mood said, 'This Pulasa fish tastes like none other. Purna, make sure you learn this dish. You can impress your would-be husband and keep him under your control just as your mother does to your father.' He poked Mitrajit with his elbow as he said that.

'Can't argue with that statement,' Mitrajit took upon the jab from his friend to lighten up the room.

'I am not going to learn that dish as I don't want to get married and leave,' Purna announced, unhappy at having the discussion of her marriage brought up. Looking at Arochan, she continued, 'Even you are laughing at this, braathaa. I thought you were on my side.'

'Of course, I am on your side dear,' Arochan replied. 'Let us please not discuss controlling husbands with the Pulasa dish. Let Purna decide which dish she wants to learn through which she can handle her husband.'

Everyone burst into laughter. Purna, sitting in between Mitrajit and Arochan, turned towards Arochan and started hitting him.

44

Arochan continued to laugh as he enjoyed teasing Purna. Since childhood they both grew up together and were supportive of each other. Though they loved and cared for each other as siblings, Arochan enjoyed teasing Purna once in a while for fun.

'Don't worry, Purna. These men always try to tease us as if we boss around, but they know that they are the kings of the house.' Subhadra tried to intervene and support Purna. She always longed for a girl child but due to health complications couldn't conceive another child after Arochan. For her, Purna was the daughter she never gave birth to.

'Hey, I never boss around at the house,' Chitraangad replied with a wink. Everyone had a good laugh at that as they knew how Chitraangad would dominate most discussions.

'By the way, how are your Jyotishya studies going on, Purna?' Arochan tried to change the topic and discuss something that Purna was always excited about. He knew how passionate she was about the subject and always encouraged her. He himself was interested in Ganitam[39] but never got a chance to dig deeper as he had to learn Dhanurveda[40] and focus on khadga vidya[41].

'I am enjoying it, braathaa. Acharya has been teaching us about the yagnas this term and I look forward to seeing how the chithi will

[39] Mathematics

[40] Military skills

[41] Sword fighting

be organized at tomorrow's yagna. But I also miss my khadga vidya as pitashri and you all have been out for a few weeks.'

'Don't worry, Purna. We will get back to our sessions once we come back,' Arochan said, reassuring her. Purna nodded and gave a smile. She knew he was saying that to make her feel better while praying quietly that his words should come true.

*****

By the time Mitrajit reached the temple along with Purna and Dhruti, he saw Aparajit and Kumudini already sitting on the platform, along with the acharya, to start the yagna processes. Arochan was helping the acharya with arranging materials on the platform needed for the yagna. All the men were sitting on one side of the platform below on a mat and women and kids were on the other side.

Mitrajit looked at Dhruti and said, 'This is one thing I can never understand as to why men and women sit separately at these occasions. Because of this, I never get to sit beside you unless we are the ones performing the pooja.'

Dhruti gave a smile and said, 'You know what? Let us sit together today. I know people may look at us questionably, but I hope they will understand. This is not any other occasion. This could be the last time we as a family are participating in a yagna together. I hope others will also follow us.' Without saying anything further, she took his hand and moved to the middle of the mat and sat down, pulling him and Purna down onto the mat.

Mitrajit looked at her and gave a smile. He was so proud of her. This was not a day to differentiate on who sat where based on gender. This was a day to pray together and spend time together. He looked towards the platform and saw Aparajit posing a smile as a sign to approve of what they had just done. Aparajit was a reasonable chieftain who would very much look at things with a balance for tradition and appropriateness.

Chitraangad along with Subhadra came and sat behind Mitrajit and family. Within minutes they could see how every other family started sitting together. Chitraangad slowly bent forwards towards Mitrajit and Dhruti and said, 'You definitely did start a revolution and hope it didn't ruffle the feathers of the acharya.'

After the yagna, Aparajit got up and raised his hand to have everyone lower their voices and concentrate on his announcement. 'Ustrakarnikas from Devasthana and beyond, thank you for joining us today for this yagna. We have prayed for the prosperity and safety of our tribe, and we hope Lord Shiva blesses us accordingly. As you all know, these are challenging times for us as a tribe and as a region. As per our ally Kalinga kingdom's request, all able Ustrakarnika men will leave tomorrow morning by sunrise. Gather along at the chatvaram tomorrow and we will continue our onward journey towards Kurukshetra. Remember it will take more than a few days to travel as we need to cover almost a hundred yojanas[42] to reach the battlefield. We will first meet with the Kalinga army at the training camp across the Vindhyas and continue our onward journey together with them.'

'I can assure the women, kids and elders of our tribe that we have kept enough resources for you all in our barns,' Aparajit continued. 'I have arranged for regular patrolling which will be conducted by some of our elders led by Mareechi who will see to it that you are all safe during our absence. I know we can't know the outcome of this war, but if some of us do not come back you can be confident to know that we will have fought our best in the war. May Lord Shiva bless us all.'

Mitrajit was holding Dhruti's hand all through the announcement. His mind was filled with love and affection for her and Purna while the cloud of an unknown future settled over him.

That evening, Mitrajit packed all his stuff in his bag while Purna helped him condition his leather shoes and scabbard. Dhruti cooked and packed for the next day's journey along with some fruits.

Just before dinner time, Dhruti brought a bright yellow cloth for Mitrajit to pack. It was a long cloth with intricately designed blue imprints. 'I have been keeping this turban as a surprise for you to wear for Purna's marriage. Now that I don't know when that will happen, I wanted to see you wear this tomorrow morning as you go

---

[42] A unit of distance. About 10 to 15 kilometers

to the war.' She looked down to the ground as she spoke those words. She didn't want Mitrajit to look at her teary eyes.

Looking at her, he raised her face with his two palms under her cheeks. Her eyes were wet, and he took a deep breath to control his own emotions. 'I don't want to wear it tomorrow as I want to have the hope that I will come back to wear it at her wedding. But if you want me to wear it tomorrow, then I will,' he said.

'Oh no, swami. I was foolish to ask you to wear it tomorrow. Please forgive me,' she said with tears rolling down her pink cheeks. Mitrajit wiped her tears and gave her a hug. 'I understand, Dhruti. It is a lot of emotional turmoil for us. All I want is to keep the hope of coming back safely. Don't worry, it is going to be all okay with Lord Shiva's blessings,' his hug became a bit tighter as he said that.

*****

Devasthana arose to a cloudy day. The sad mood around the village turned much gloomier with the early morning fog. Mitrajit woke up to see Purna already awake. She had gone into the backyard to collect flowers. She tied them together into a garland. 'Get ready pitashri, we will quickly pray before you head out. I already cleaned up the pooja altar,' she said. She always used to look for opportunities to avoid cleaning up and setting up the pooja altar, but not today.

After the prayer, Purna put the garland she prepared around Mitrajit. Dhruti took the sacred ashes from the altar and applied them on Mitrajit's forehead before taking the vermillion and applied the tilakam. Mitrajit hugged his family. He didn't want to leave the hug, but eventually got up with a big sigh. He put on his armor, slung his bag over his shoulder, took his shield and sword, and headed out of his home with Purna and Dhruti following him.

Everyone started to gather near the chatvaram with families gathered to bid goodbye to their men. Men from other villages also arrived early in the morning to join the Ustrakarnika unit.

Aparajit was talking to the elder Mareechi to finalize security plans. It was important that Devasthana and other villages were protected from any transgressions from the Ekapaadas during their absence. Chitraangad was in high spirits talking to the rest of the men while Arochan joined them along with Subhadra.

Subhadra's face showed the emotions that reflected the mood of the other villagers that morning. She looked petrified at the prospect of her husband and son going to the war. She was not the only woman among the villagers to be in that position but was the only one not hiding her emotions.

She didn't want to leave her son's hand even for a second. 'I don't know how other mothers are accepting to send their young sons to this war. Will Prince Arjuna's wife Subhadra be willing to send their son Abhimanyu into the war?' she asked during the dinner the other night when Arochan and Purna were not in the room. Chitraangad replied boisterously, 'Of course she would. With a son as brave as Abhimanyu, who wouldn't? And my son is not any lesser than

Abhimanyu. He has learnt all the skills needed and this war is a good exposure for him to apply what he has learned.'

'I don't know what she will do. Maybe I am not as brave as that Subhadra. Maybe I am selfish in thinking that I want my son to be safe. This is not any battle with the Ekapaadas and my heart pains at the thought of sending off my son to this war,' she replied that day.

Even on this day, Subhadra's facial expressions showed that she would give anything to make her son avoid going into this war. Dhruti came to her and hugged her. Tears rolled down Subhadra's cheeks.

'Ah. Don't cry now. Send me and your son with a smile. We just prayed to bless us to be victorious,' Chitraangad said, looking at her. In a mood not to argue with him, Subhadra wiped her tears and put on a forced smile on her face.

Mitrajit went to her and replied, 'Apart from Chitra, I will also be around to protect Arochan. You can be assured that as long as his father and uncle are with him, no harm will approach him.' Those words gave some confidence to Subhadra.

The loud sound from the conch brought all of them to reality. Aparajit had just blown the conch to announce their departure. Everyone started arranging themselves in an orderly form. Aparajit, with Chitraangad and Mitrajit on his side, announced, 'Namaskaram, everyone. It is time for the able men of our great Ustrakarnika tribe to join the biggest war ever fought on Bharata varsha. They say this war will be a doom for the wrong side and a boon for the right side. I cannot say if we are on the right side because every side may be feeling the same. But one thing is sure, if we fight this war with the right attitude and righteousness, we will leave the war as winners. Please do pray for us and keep the hope of seeing your dear ones soon. Until then, may Lord Shiva bless us all.'

As the men moved towards the outskirts of the village, they were followed by their families until the village gate. Mitrajit turned to look back at Dhruti and Purna and saw them looking down with sad faces. Purna looked towards the moving unit and saw that her father was looking at them. 'Amma, keep smiling, pitashri is looking at us,' she said. Dhruti got shaken up from her thoughts and saw Mitrajit looking at them. She waved at him, bringing her smile back. She wanted to make sure Mitrajit left on high spirits. She was happy to see Purna was mature enough to understand the situation.

Mitrajit raised his hand to give one final wave. He then turned around and started walking ahead towards the forest.

*****

'We need to pace ourselves to continue for at least two yojanas at a stretch before taking any break. This way we can also make up for time lost due to wading moonlight,' Aparajit said to Chitraangad and Mitrajit. They both nodded in agreement and communicated with the men behind them to catch up with their pace.

They took breaks in between to refresh and stretch before continuing further. During one of the breaks, Aparajit made an announcement to his men. 'We are going to meet the Kalinga and

Anga armies at the training camp. Once we reach there, we will have more updates, but as far as I am told we will be fighting alongside them under the Kalinga's King Srutayush command.'

Aparajit was an astute leader who had respect from all the Ustrakarnikas. It was not easy to survive as a tribe without being part of a kingdom. For many generations, Aparajit's family had been leading the tribe with strategic alliances in the region and he continued the tradition. He knew when to connect diplomatically with other kingdoms. With the Ekapaadas continuously attacking their boundaries, it was his idea to ally with the Kalinga kingdom that helped them to keep Ekapaadas at bay.

Meanwhile, Chitraangad seemed excited during the journey northward. He always enjoyed opportunities to showcase his swordsmanship. 'What is the use of learning a skill if you don't use it?' he would always say to Mitrajit.

'Here it is. Our chance to shine and get to showcase our talents amongst the mighty warriors of Bharata varsha,' Chitraangad said as they continued in the evening. He always had a positive outlook on things. Ever since childhood, he and Mitrajit had been the best of friends; they were more like brothers. Chitraangad was a single son just like him and both of their parents were close friends too.

Mitrajit smiled back and said, 'Yes, now that we are on our way anyway, let us give our best shot. Friends forever, brothers always.' That was their rallying cry whenever they would fight back the Ekapaadas.

*****

As the men crossed the fields and moved up into the woods, the mist slowly filled up the gap between the men and the villagers. Dhruti and Purna took a deep breath and started going back home. Subhadra was behind them with Kumudini.

Mareechi went towards Kumudini and said, 'I will connect with the rest of the elders and create a patrolling routine so that we can alert you all in case of any incursions in the south. Meanwhile, please do not hesitate to call us for any assistance.'

'Thank you, Uncle,' Kumudini said as she continued. She saw that the rest of the women and kids were silently walking towards their homes. She felt a climate of despair in the village already. She stopped and turned back. 'Uncle Mareechi, one more thing. Can you please tell everyone to gather in the evening at the chatvaram? I cannot continue to see this mood of our villagers. When the men left for the training camp the mood was similar, but now it looks like even their morale is low. We need to keep up the spirits of everyone as we wait for our men to come back. I will have an announcement at that time.'

'Very good point, my lady. May you be blessed for such noble thoughts,' he said while gesturing with his two hands to bless her.

MANU NELLUTLA

Even before reaching the gate of their home, Purna said, 'Can I not go to gurukul[43] today, amma? I am not in a mood to go and study today.'

Dhruti looked at her and nodded. 'Okay. But only for today. You need to continue your studies. Remember, they are very important.'

'Of course, amma. I will go back tomorrow. I am just not in a good mood with pitashri and others going to the war. I would like to go and spend time with Bhumi and Suvarna. They must be feeling sad too. I will be back by lunch time, though, to help you cook.'

Dhruti nodded in agreement. How could she not agree? Everyone would be feeling the same and even she was not in a mood to continue with her morning chores. Now that Mitrajit had gone to the war, Dhruti felt the need to express herself. She went in front of the pooja altar and cried her heart out. She had been trying to keep all the tension to herself without expressing it to Mitrajit for the past few days.

She felt better after getting all the tears out. She then realized the reason why Purna wanted to go out. Purna wanted to check on her friends. *How thoughtful of her,* she thought. She felt guilty for not checking in with Subhadra.

Poor Subhadra, she must be struggling with both her husband and young son gone to the war. Should I go and check on her or give her time to reflect and have some personal time for herself?

---

[43] School

55

Dhruti deliberated for a few seconds before deciding to go ahead to meet Subhadra.

On the way to Subhadra's house, Dhruti came across Mareechi, who was going around to communicate Kumudini's message to connect at the chatvaram. She wondered what it could be about. *Possibly Subhadra knows,* she thought.

Dhruti knocked on the door and waited. Meanwhile, she turned around and saw Purna talking to her friends at the corner of the street under a tree.

If a grown-up like me is struggling at the thought of the outcome of this war, what would be going on the kids' minds? she thought.

'Good to see you, Dhruti.' Dhruti was startled back to reality by Subhadra's voice. She turned back to see Subhadra standing with the two doors wide open. She looked tired. She must have cried too, Dhruti thought as she looked at her eyes.

'Ah. I just wanted to check on how you've been doing? I can see that you must have had a round of breakdown already,' Dhruti said with a little smile to make the mood more casual.

'Yes, just as you must have,' Subhadra replied with a smile.

It was then that Dhruti realized. She never thought that others could easily identify her state of mind too by looking at her face. She should have at least washed her face before coming here. But then, who else to share the concerns with than with friends.

'Ha-ha. Well, I felt good after it,' Dhruti replied.

'Agreed. Me too. Come inside. You know what, let's sit in the backyard. It will be cooler in the afternoon, and we can have lunch there. I was not in the mood to eat alone at home today. Glad you came,' Subhadra replied as she went into the house.

Dhruti looked towards Purna and waved. Purna was busy talking. Dhruti shouted to get her attention. Purna looked at her and signed with her hands to ask what was it about? Dhruti showed with her hand that she was going to be here. Purna nodded.

Subhadra was waiting for Dhruti. 'What happened? Didn't Purna go to gurukul today?' she inquired.

Dhruti answered, 'No. She wasn't in a mood today. She wanted to connect with her friends and check upon them to see if they are fine. It's good that they have each other's support.'

'Just as we have each other,' Subhadra replied with a smile.

Dhruti nodded with a smile back. 'By the way, what is the gathering about that Kumudini was mentioning to Mareechi?' she asked.

'Oh. She wanted to plan a few activities over the next couple of days so that we could keep the villagers engaged. I think that is a good idea.'

'Absolutely!' Dhruti replied.

During lunch, Subhadra asked Purna. 'So, how are your friends doing?'

'They are all okay. We understand that during times of war there are always uncertainties, but we will be fine. There is lots to work on our assignments given by acharya, so we better concentrate on that.' Purna replied.

'Good thing. It will keep you all engaged and diverted from the thoughts of the warfront,' Subhadra replied. She then looked at Dhruti with her eyebrow elevated as in surprise. Dhruti understood that expression of Subhadra. She must have been surprised at the maturity that Purna was displaying

After lunch, they were joined by Kumudini. 'I was thinking of arranging a few events over the next couple of days to lift the spirit of the villagers. On one day we could have vanabhojanam[44], one evening could be a khadga vidya demonstration by kids, one evening could be Ramayana sermon, and one day could be Goddess Tulasi pooja. What do you think?' she asked.

'Those are all wonderful ideas, Kumudini. Very thoughtful. I think it will help us keep our minds distracted from the thoughts of the war,' Dhruti replied.

'I agree. It will give something for everyone - kids, women, and elders - to participate in these events. I know our men will appreciate the fact that we're not in a despaired mood when they're not around this time,' Subhadra followed up with her thought on Kumudini's ideas.

In the evening, everyone at the chatvaram received these ideas warmly. Mareechi shouted from the crowd, 'This is the best thing I have heard in a few days.' Everybody agreed in unison.

---

[44] Having lunch as a group under a tree/in garden

'Thank you. Now let us start with the Ramayana sermon tomorrow evening.' Kumudini was excited to have the villagers receive her ideas positively.

*****

With the pace they were keeping up, Aparajit felt confident of reaching the training camp sooner than expected. Chitraangad kept everyone at task to keep up with the pace. He was always ready to help Aparajit with managing the day-to-day affairs of Devasthana.

Mitrajit was able to get some rest that evening before crossing the pass in between the Vindhya mountains. After he was done with his routine evening meditation, Mitrajit enjoyed the dishes packed by Dhruti. *She was so considerate and thoughtful in the way she packed,* he thought. She wrote on each pack what the dish was and when to eat it. She wanted to make it easy for him. The training and military camps were very well planned to ensure soldiers are well fed with nutritious meals to ensure they were getting good nourishment, but nothing could beat home cooked food.

'Thanks for assuring Subhadra that we will take care of Arochan.' Chitraangad said while opening his own pack of food. Mitrajit looked at his friend and smiled. Mitrajit always considered Arochan as his own nephew. It was Mitrajit who helped his friend choose the name for his son. Arochan at seventeen was a bright young man with a radiant glow on his face, just as Mitrajit saw him when he was born thus justifying his choice for the name, the one with exuberant radiance.

Both Mitrajit and Chitraangad were impressed with the way Arochan had learnt Dhanurveda while excelling in sword fighting skills. He was brave and never hesitated to take the first strike. Mitrajit could understand why his friend was feeling proud to go into the battle front with his son beside him. At the same time, Mitrajit also understood the worried look on Subhadra's face. No mother would like having her young son go into a war where you they were fighting along with the mightiest warriors the Bharata varsha had ever seen. But Mitrajit was confident that between him and Chitraangad, they could ensure that Arochan was well protected, even during the battles.

It could have been the early start for the day or the continuous trudging through the forests that made Mitrajit doze off into deep sleep as soon as he hit his mat. Even the noises from the crickets and frogs didn't bother him. He woke up in the morning only when Chitraangad shook him to awaken him.

'Looks like someone had a very good night's sleep. Rise and shine my friend. We don't want to be late,' Chitraangad said as he took a conch to blow the horn to gather attention of the unit.

'We will leave in the next ghadiya. We are pacing well. We should be there by late evening,' Aparajit announced.

It was cooler in the morning but started getting warmer by the afternoon, thus slowing down the unit. Chitraangad looked at

Mitrajit and said, 'Did you notice how our unit has split into two groups going at different paces?'

Mitrajit didn't understand and looked at Chitraangad with a questioning look on his face.

'If you haven't noticed, there is a group in front of us pacing faster than us and that group consists of mostly youngsters. We are now officially in the group of older people pacing slowly,' Chitraangad quipped.

Mitrajit gave a look at the group in front of them and saw youngsters like Arochan walking quicker than others. He looked around and saw Aparajit, Ravi and Viraata. The older men were sweating as they were trying to keep up the pace. Mitrajit laughed his heart out and said, 'You are funny, Chitra.'

They both had a good laugh. The next part of the journey was relatively easier for them as it was mostly downhill, taking them to the valley where the training camp was located. Mitrajit observed there were more tents laid out at the camp this time than a few days back when they were there. In anticipation of other Kaurava allied units joining this time, he assumed.

Aparajit and the Ustrakarnikas arrived at the training camp one ghadiya earlier than expected. Once closer to the camp, a guard with the Kalinga insignia on his armor came towards Aparajit and the chieftain handed over his credentials to them to confirm.

After getting an update from the guard, Aparajit looked towards his unit and said, 'General Pattabhadra from the Kalinga army will show you all the arrangements they made for us at the camp. He will be our main contact for day-to-day operations. I will connect with other commanders of the Kalinga and get back to you with any new information.'

After the announcement, Aparajit went inside a huge, heavily guarded tent. *It must be where important people or royalty are staying,* Mitrajit thought.

'Greetings, Ustrakarnikas. I am General Pattabhadra from the Kalinga Army. Welcome back to the training camp. Please follow me and I will show you to your tents.' General Pattabhadra said in his deep baritone voice as he gestured his hand towards the camp site.

On the way to their tents, Mitrajit and Chitraangad introduced themselves to General Pattabhadra. 'Oh yes, Aparajit said that you two are his closest aides. Please do ask me if you have any questions as we plan for the battles too,' Pattabhadra replied.

Chitraangad was curious to ask, 'Did the Anga army along with the mighty King Karna arrive at the campsite?'

'Not yet. We heard that they would reach Kurukshetra directly. We are here along with our King Srutayush who will be briefing all of us before dinner. He is currently meeting with other commanders and your chieftain is there in that meeting.'

'That is interesting! Any idea why they were going directly to Kurukshetra?' Mitrajit asked.

'I am sorry, but I don't have any more information. Maybe we will get more information later. I will update you if I get to know more.' With that reply, Pattabhadra turned towards the campsite and signaled everyone to follow him.

Mitrajit couldn't help but notice a slight limp in Pattabhadra's gait. *May be an injury from a previous battle,* he thought. He remembered how his own father had a similar limp since getting injured in one of the skirmishes with the Ekapaadas.

After showing the campsite for the Ustrakarnikas, Pattabhadra said, 'Please settle down and refresh yourselves. Be at the central site of the training camp in two ghadiyas for the announcement from the king. I will see you there.'

Everyone took their spot under the tents. Mitrajit excused himself from the others to meditate. If there was time before the announcement, he thought he'd better complete his routine.

After meditation, Mitrajit came to chat with Chitraangad who seemed busy talking with Arochan. By the looks of the expressions, it seemed as if Chitraangad was discussing how to tackle an attack from archers. *No matter how much advanced training Arochan has had, Chitraangad will have something to add to ensure his son is aware and be safe,* Mitrajit thought.

For a moment, his thoughts went back to Dhruti and Purna. As it was almost dinner time, Mitrajit thought they may be cooking together, with Dhruti ensuring Purna helped and Purna playing one of her tantrums. He let out a small smile at that thought.

*****

At the sound of the conch being blown, Mitrajit and the others went towards the central site of the camp. All the Ustrakarnikas, in thousands, stood together on one side of the platform which was put up in the middle. Beside them were various units from the Kalinga army with shiva linga on their body armors. On the platform was Aparajit, standing along with other commanders of the Kalinga kingdom.

General Pattabhadra came towards Mitrajit and Chitraangad and said, 'Good to see you, my friends. You are just in time for the announcement.'

Pointing at the people on the platform, Pattabhadra mentioned each person's name. 'The two commanders beside Aparajit are Ketumanta and Bhanumanta, the brothers of our King Srutayush. To their right is King Srutayush and to his right is his son Prince Sakradeva. To the right of Prince Sakradeva are commanders from our other allies, the Pulindas.'

'Thank you,' Mitrajit replied. He looked up towards the platform and noticed Aparajit looking at him. Aparajit nodded, acknowledging that he had seen the unit arrive for debrief.

Prince Sakradeva came to the front of the platform and raised his hand up. He looked to be in his thirties, and there was a confident look in the prince's face.

Everyone stood quietly for the announcement. 'Good evening, everyone. For our friends who joined us, my name is Sakradeva. We are happy that you all have joined us at this camp including our friends from the south, the Ustrakarnikas, and our friends from the west, the Pulindas. We also got an update that our friend and ally, King Karna along with his Anga army will be joining us directly at the battlefront. Now please welcome with cheers, our mighty King Srutayush to grace us with his speech.'

'So, the mighty kings only grace us with speeches,' Chitraangad quipped while whispering to Mitrajit.

'Ssshhh…,' Mitrajit was trying hard not to laugh at his friend's joke.

Everyone started cheering and applauding as King Srutayush came forward. He hugged his son and turned towards the crowd. He waved his hand and turned around so that he could wave towards the soldiers on the other side of the platform too.

Wearing a dazzling armor with the linga insignia and with the war helmet on his head, King Srutayush looked grand as he stood tall on the platform.

He raised his hand again as a signal to quiet down his units. He then took a deep breath and started his speech.

'Greetings, everyone. May Lord Vyaghreswara[45] bless us all. I feel fortunate to be participating in this war with all you brave soldiers, including my brothers and son. This war is not any ordinary war. This is a war where the rightful heir to the Kuru Kingdom will be appointed king. Our friend Duryodhana has asked us to support him in his quest to defeat the Pandavas once and for all and confirm his place as the king. It is his right since his father is the current king. It is our chance to fight along with our friends and show the Pandavas that Duryodhana has his friends to count on.'

---

[45] Another name for Lord Shiva.

'Talking about friends, thanks to the Ustrakarnikas and the Pulindas for joining us. Our alliance is as strong as the mighty rivers Godavari and Mahanadi flowing through our lands. Us along with the mighty King Karna and his strong Anga army will definitely show the Pandavas what taking on Duryodhana and his friends is like.'

'The last time you were at the training camp, you must have gotten a chance to practice all the vyuhas that may be utilized at the war. Prince Sakradeva will be working with your commanders and chieftains during the war to ensure you get your orders directly and quickly. We all are going to be part of one big akshauhini unit and I am confident that we will wreak havoc on the Pandavas. Our strong elephant unit will be hard for them to crack open.'

'We will be leaving early in the morning and pace ourselves so that we can reach Kurukshetra in the next two to three days. Our elephant unit has already moved ahead, and it will be easier to move through the forests as the elephant unit must have already cleared the way for us through the woods. But for now, let us leave the thoughts of tomorrow's journey. First let us enjoy our dinner. We also have lots of Paisti[46] and Gaudi[47] for you today. It may be a long time before we can enjoy the drinks again. So, go ahead and enjoy. I will see you in the battlefront. Jai[48] Vyaghreswara.' With that, King

---

[46] Grain fermented alcoholic drink like beer

[47] Alcoholic drink fermented from jaggery

[48] Hail.

Srutayush ended his speech. All his army units erupted in unison, shouting Jai Vyaghreswara, the battle cry for the Kalingas.

'Oh, that was a great speech,' Pattabhadra said, looking at Mitrajit and Chitraangad. 'Our king always inspires us. Please come join me for dinner and drinks,' he said as he showed towards the other side of the mound hinting that's where the dinner would be arranged.

'Absolutely. Thank you,' Chitraangad replied, looking at Mitrajit.

'Thanks for the invitation. Is Aparajit or others from our unit joining us too?' Mitrajit asked. He was also feeling hesitant to spend time with such a high general of the Kalinga army.

'Your chieftain will be having dinner with the other commanders and royalty. I think it is important for them to connect with each other. Same reason I am here with you. I hope your men also mingle with other Kalingas and Pulindas. We are going to fight together in this war, so what better way to know each other well than getting together for drinks?' Pattabhadra replied.

'Agreed,' Mitrajit replied. *Makes sense,* he thought to himself.

'Also, please inform your men to leave their shields outside your tents. Our men will get them decked with our insignia paint for easier identification in the battle front as we fight as one akshauhini,' Pattabhadra informed.

Chitraangad went to communicate with others in the unit. 'Please go ahead, mingle and enjoy your dinner. Before you go, please ensure you keep your shields outside the tent so that they can be painted with insignia. Now remember, don't be too late as we need to wake up early for our move towards Kurukshetra. Arochan will be with you all as myself and Mitrajit will be joining General Pattabhadra.'

Chitraangad would always step up whenever Aparajit was not around, and the units were aware that Chitraangad had been groomed to take over as the next chieftain once Aparajit retired, as the current chieftain didn't have any heir of his own.

'Make sure none of them consume a lot of alcohol, and you behave well too. Don't go too crazy with your friends,' he said to Arochan.

'Poor boy. He must be eager to be with his friends and enjoy. Let him,' Mitrajit told Chitraangad as they both followed Pattabhadra.

'Ah. Uncle to the rescue,' Chitraangad replied laughing. 'I am so looking forward to the dinner and drinks,' he said.

After leaving their shields outside the tent, Mitrajit and Chitraangad followed General Pattabhadra towards the dinner tent. There were huge pots filled with alcohol. People were lined up with small glasses to fill them up.

As they sat down to have their drinks, Chitraangad asked Pattabhadra, 'So what do you think about this war and the outcome?'

'Well, all we can say is that as soldiers all we do is follow the orders of our commanders. I follow my commanders and my soldiers follow mine. We cannot question what the kings and princes have determined. At the end of the day, being a soldier pays us enough to keep our families sustained,' the general answered.

'True that,' Chitraangad continued. 'We all have different reasons and priorities to participate in this war. What about Krishna's participation? Sorry for asking more questions. I am curious. Because his participation alone could change the outcome of this war.'

'Well, we heard that Krishna is not participating directly in the war. Instead, he is going to be the charioteer for Arjuna while his army, the dreaded Narayani sena has been promised to fight along the Kauravas side against the Pandavas. I don't know how that works, but we will see.' The general replied with a shrug.

'That's interesting for sure. But we will see how that turns out at the war. For now, all I want is another glass of Paisti,' Chitraangad said as he got up to fill his glass.

After the drinks, they all went back to their tents. Mitrajit observed that some of their shields were already painted and put out to dry out.

'Age is definitely creeping up. I couldn't drink more than three glasses of Paisti.' Chitraangad said with a smile. 'Time to sleep now. It's been a long day,' he said as he stretched his body before lying down on the bed.

Long day for sure, Mitrajit thought. He himself was feeling sleepy after two glasses of Gaudi. With Chitraangad almost ready to sleep, Mitrajit checked around the tent to make sure Arochan was back with the rest of the troops.

Mitrajit was about to sleep when he saw Aparajit coming into the tent to take his position on the mat to sleep. *He must have had a busy evening of meetings*, Mitrajit thought.

Mitrajit had never been any further north than the Vindhya mountains. He was curious about what the war front would look like. He also was visualizing how the war front would look like. They have been in small battles against the Ekapaadas but never in a full-fledged battle. He was curious about how big the battle zone could be.

As his thoughts were meandering, Mitrajit's eyes felt heavier and heavier. He slowly started thinking about Dhruti and Purna. When can I see them again? Will I live to see them again? Mitrajit went into deep sleep with thoughts and dreams about his family.

4.Smriti[49] Parva

As Mitrajit went deep into sleep, he dreamt about a time from few months earlier.

Purna asked curiously, 'Pitashri, how come we are not part of any kingdom?', as they walked towards their farm to harvest the vegetables to be sold at the Friday market.

Their farm wasn't very big, but it was sufficient to grow different vegetables in different seasons. Changing the types of vegetables in various seasons also kept the soil fertile. From the sale of the vegetables for the past two years, Mitrajit was able to get enough resources to repair the roof and fence around their home. Part of

---

[49] Memories

their earnings would go to the city taxes which were collected by Aparajit who in turn would contribute it to Kalinga Kingdom's treasury as part of their alliance agreement.

Mitrajit encouraged Purna to ask questions. 'A curious mind is a learning mind,' he would say whenever Dhruti would complain about Purna's questioning.

Mitrajit was happy that Purna asked questions to understand the political landscape. She seemed intrigued by the way the Pandavas were treated by the Kauravas though she was clever enough to say that Yudhishthira shouldn't have played the game of dice and even if he wanted to, he shouldn't have made a bet on his brothers, wife, and kingdom. *True that*, Mitrajit thought. He never understood the way these kings and princes think and conduct.

'Well, we don't have huge lands with us to be considered a kingdom. Also, since we are small, no one thought yet of taking over our region to make it part of their kingdom. Which I think in one way is advantageous too as we remain independent. At the same time, our ancestors were so good at fighting that they thwarted all attempts made by Ekapaadas just as we have been trying to. I also think our geographical location also helps us. Big armies prefer to fight in open grounds and battle fronts; whereas our location creates obstacles for them and helps us fight them locally with our small units,' he said while plucking the brinjals.

'At the same time, I think if we were part of a kingdom, we would be protected all along and no one would dare to attack us,' Purna replied.

'That is a good point but imagine this. We would not have all the freedom we want to. We'd have to follow what the king would say, and our culture could be lost in the big plans for the kingdom. Whereas being independent while in an alliance helps in both being free while being safe,' Chitraangad tried to justify his reasoning further.

'Yes. The only caveat is that being in an alliance means you may be called up into unwanted battles that you don't want to be part of,' Purna replied.

'Well interesting point, Purna. So far, we have not been in that situation yet.'

Mitrajit was glad to see Purna's reasoning skills in the discussions. But Purna's curiosity would sometimes lead to disagreements with Dhruti. She would always ask her mother why only girls had to learn all the household chores. 'Does Arochan braathaa also has to learn all these chores?' she asked once.

Though Dhruti didn't believe that Purna should only learn household chores, she believed it would be good for her daughter and her future family if Purna learnt how to cook and maintain home properly.

Mitrajit also always wanted to ensure Purna wasn't seen as a girl child who was only confined to the household chores. He and Dhruti promised themselves to teach her everything, including weapons training. He, along with Arochan, also spent a couple of hours every week to teach her khadga vidya.

Everyone in Devasthana appreciated the way Mitrajit encouraged Purna to learn other skills. Some of them also started teaching their daughters sword fighting skills. They recognized it was important for women of the tribe to learn similar skills to the men to defend Devasthana and other villages in situations of need.

Aparajit was very supportive of this. He often used the example of Satyabhama, who was married to Dwarka's Krishna, to encourage more families to teach their girl child military skills. Satyabhama accompanied Krishna in his war against Narakasura of Pragjotishpura and killed him in the battle.

Dhruti appreciated the intent of Mitrajit to encourage Purna to learn different skills. She herself never had the chance of learning any of the martial arts as she was encouraged to concentrate on household chores in her childhood. When she got married to Mitrajit, it was a huge change as he was more open for her to learn things that men would do, including ploughing and khadga vidya. He wanted her to be independent in case something happened to him.

Mitrajit got disturbed for a few minutes from his sleep as he heard patrol guards walking outside the tent. *Even training camps full of soldiers need guards*, he thought as he turned to side and slowly went back to sleep.

*****

It was during his childhood that Mitrajit first heard about the Ekapaadas. His mother, Revati, used to share stories about how the Ustrakarnikas were able to hold their defenses against the Ekapaadas. He used to appreciate how the stories highlighted Ustrakarnikas as a peace-loving tribe, but one that wouldn't hesitate to fight till their last breath to defend their tribe if needed.

His dreams continued to take him to that one night which had left a mark on his mind for years to come.

It was a few days after his sixth birthday during the Uttarayana[50]. While everyone was sleeping, his father, Vamadeva, woke him up from his sleep and signaled him to be quiet. 'Shh. Don't make any sound. Our village has been surrounded by the Ekapaadas. Some of our men are fighting at the border of the village to stop them from coming in. Come quickly with me,' he said.

Mitrajit was terrified hearing about the Ekapaadas. His friends used to say that the Ekapaadas were dark skinned and turban wearing, with ash smeared all over their bodies. He used to imagine them as the mythological rakshasas who would attack priests and saints in the forests during prabhu Ram's time.

Vamadeva took Mitrajit and Revati to his close friend, Rayvanth's home. By the time they got there, Rayvanth was already at the stairs with his sword in hand and a lantern in another.

'Get inside quickly. Vani and Chitraangad are sitting in the common room,' he said. Mitrajit recalled how Rayvanth had a unique

---

[50] Winter Solstice.

moustache which almost covered his cheeks. He used to fear Rayvanth when he was much younger, but once he became acquainted with his father's friend, Mitrajit grew out of it.

Mitrajit ran into the common room to talk to his friend Chitraangad. They both used to talk about how the Ekapaadas would look and how once they grew up, they will destroy the Ekapaadas.

'Do you know what is going to happen?' Mitrajit asked Chitraangad as soon as he saw him.

'Oh, don't you worry. My father along with your father will crush those Ekapaadas like ants. You know my father forged a special sword last week. He is going to use it to cut off their heads and arms,' Chitraangad replied in his usual bravado.

'Turn off all the lamps. Close the door and keep your swords ready in case they cross us and come towards the home,' Rayvanth said as he stepped outside the house along with Vamadeva.

Mitrajit and Chitraangad sat close to the window, and they could see shadows of men fighting at the village fence. They could hear the clashing of the swords and screams from the southern side. They both slept near the window as the fighting went on into the dawn.

Just after sunrise, Mitrajit and Chitraangad were woken up from their sleep by the sudden opening of the door. They looked over and saw Vamadeva with blood oozing from the front of his thigh. He had a makeshift bandage with his turban tied around this thigh to stop the bleeding.

Behind his father, Mitrajit saw Rayvanth's body fully covered in blood. He had blood dripping from his head, arms and back. Aparajit and Mareechi were holding Rayvanth as they brought him inside the house.

The vaidya[51] came running behind them with some bandages. Chitraangad was in shock to see his father injured and bleeding. Not knowing what to do, he went and hugged his mom and started crying.

Mitrajit went towards his friend and hugged him. 'Don't worry. The vaidya is here and he is putting on the bandages. He will be fine,' he said, reassuring his friend.

'The Ekapaadas are crushed. They will not dare to attack us for a few years after the loss they have made. They won't dare come towards Devasthana again.' Rayvanth was talking loudly as the vaidya attended to him and tried to stop the bleeding.

'Rayvanth. Don't talk. You need to rest. Yes, we have defeated them for now and I'm glad that you are still alive,' Vamadeva said.

The vaidya also attended to Vamadeva's injury and applied bandage to his thigh wound. 'It will heal in a few days, but the cut is deep.' Mitrajit heard the vaidya talking to his father.

'No problem. Thanks for helping. I hope my friend will be fine soon.' Vamadeva asked.

Before even the vaidya could answer, Rayvanth replied, 'Oh, I am fine. Thanks to Lord Shiva's blessings. I am glad we could push them back.'

---

[51] Doctor/medic

'Of course. Now you both need to rest well. I will get back to work on mending the fences and trenches. The Ekapaadas may have been defeated for now but you never know when they will attack again,' Aparajit said while leaving the house.

In the coming months, Rayvanth couldn't recover from his injuries which worsened over the days with infection. He passed away after a few months. Chitraangad's mother Vani died a few days later, which everyone attributed to heartbreak. It was during this time that chieftain Aparajit, who didn't have any kids of his own, took Chitraangad under his wing. He ensured that Chitraangad got all the support needed from the villagers.

Vamadeva along with Revati also provided Chitraangad with all the support they could. This strengthened the bond and attachment between Mitrajit and Chitraangad.

*****

The wound in Vamadeva's thigh made him limp slightly all his life long. He was a strong-willed man and ensured that his disability didn't affect his chores and duties. He continued to help Aparajit with affairs of the tribe while continuing to farm. He used to tell Mitrajit, 'No matter what the trouble is, remember there is always a solution.'

Mitrajit used to like spending time with his father. Vamadeva used to tell him about the stories from various powerful dynasties in the Bharata varsha including the Kuru dynasty. Mitrajit remembered

Vamadeva telling him how Dhritarastra was responsible for taking care of his people when the actual King Pandu abdicated his throne and went away into forests with his wives. 'It is way easier to renounce or stay away from your responsibilities, but it is the duty of the brave to take up responsibilities in times of chaos,' Vamadeva said at that time.

Apart from his father and acharya at the gurukul, Mitrajit used to learn a lot about itihaasa[52] through his mother's stories. He also learnt how to meditate from his mother. His mother was privy to Aranyagaya[53] of the Samaveda[54] and used to sing melodies to get into a meditative state. It was her who stressed the importance of both physical and mental well-being.

As Mitrajit grew, he learnt various skills, but the one that he excelled most at was the khadga vidya. His acharya was so impressed with his skill that he forged a special sword as a gift for him.

Mitrajit, along with Chitraangad, trained under Aparajit to learn diplomacy and administrative works. 'I am grooming you both to help me run this place when I grow older,' Aparajit would tell them.

*****

---

[52] History.

[53] Hymns of forest

[54] One of the Vedic scriptures

When both Mitrajit and Chitraangad reached seventeen years, Vamadeva took the responsibility to start looking for suitable brides for the two young men. 'I think it will be good for them to settle down. With the Ekapaadas not the same threat to us as they used to be, this will be an apt time to let them focus on building their own families,' he said to Aparajit.

Aparajit advised Vamadeva to take the young men to the village Keertipuram which was in the Asmaka kingdom, where he heard the news that the Keertipuram chieftain, Durvasa, was looking for groom for his daughter. Vamadeva communicated with Durvasa and along with Revati took the two young men to Keertipuram.

'Looks like the days of you being a mother's boy are over,' Chitraangad teased Mitrajit when he heard about the news.

On reaching Keertipuram, Vamadeva and Durvasa met each other with their families. Mitrajit was awestruck to see Dhruti for the first time. He had never seen anyone so beautiful. Once both of their parents agreed, the marriage ceremony was held the next day.

It was during the ceremony that Chitraangad met Subhadra, the daughter of the priest of Keertipuram. Seeing both being interested in each other, Revati asked Vamadeva to approach the priest and inquire if he would be willing to give his daughter's hand to Chitraangad. 'It will be good to see both the boys getting married with girls from the same village. The girls will also not feel left out when they move with us to Devasthana,' she said.

The priest, though a bit hesitant to give his daughter to an orphan, was reminded by Vamadeva that Chitraangad was as much his son too as Mitrajit to him. Durvasa also reasoned with the priest to show how both the girls would be married into the same village and would be able to rely on each other. Seeing that both Chitraangad and Subhadra also seemed to like each other, the priest agreed for their marriage to be held the next day.

Vamadeva and Revati were so happy to see the two young men get married. Both Dhruti and Subhadra, sixteen years old at the time, were well mannered and learned. Once the ceremonies were done, they all packed up to get back to Devasthana. Vamadeva informed Durvasa and invited him and others from Keertipuram to Devasthana to attend the special yagna that he was planning in two months' time to celebrate the young men's wedding.

The happiness from the marriage ceremonies didn't last long as on their way back to Devasthana, Vamadeva and others were attacked by bandits in the Dandakaranya[55] forest. Taken by surprise, Vamadeva, Mitrajit and Chitraangad fought valiantly to counter their attack.

As Mitrajit and Chitraangad were fending off the bandits' attack, Vamadeva was guarding the newly wedded brides, Dhruti and Subhadra, along with Revati. He gave them small claw-like weapons and said, 'Wear them on your knuckles and if someone tries to approach you, hit them with this.'

---

[55] Thick forest area in ancient central India

Both Dhruti and Subhadra were shocked with the turn of events. They would have never imagined that their married life would start with danger to their own lives.

As they were fighting the bandits, Mitrajit noticed that there were at least three bandits attacking Vamadeva as he and the women were cornered near a big rock. Chitraangad was tackling two other bandits near the stream.

Mitrajit threw his shield with force on the bandit he was fighting and sliced his torso with the sword. With the bandit down, Mitrajit rushed towards his father's side. But before he could reach, one of the bandits that Vamadeva was fighting with bent down and sliced through Vamadeva's legs. Mitrajit could hear the sword crushing the bones of his father's legs. Vamadeva immediately fell to the ground. Both Dhruti and Subhadra screamed, staring at the blood flowing from Vamadeva's lower body. Revati stood still in shock, unable to fathom what had happened in front of her eyes.

Mitrajit jumped onto the bandit and kicked him from the back. The bandit fell to the ground. With no hesitation, Mitrajit took his sword and plunged it through the back of the bandit. He removed it quickly and started attacking the other two bandits. Seeing Mitrajit's rage and the fastness with which he was attacking, one of the bandits ran away. Mitrajit hit the other bandit on the head, causing him to collapse.

Before going towards his father, he turned towards the stream to ensure Chitraangad was okay. He saw that his friend had already killed one of the bandits he was fighting with and was tackling the last one.

Vamadeva was down on the ground and heavily losing the blood. He was gasping for breath. He looked feebly towards Revati.

'I think...this is it...,' Vamadeva said as he gasped for one last breath. Within seconds, Mitrajit could feel his father's body turning cold.

*****

Mitrajit suddenly woke up. This was not the first time he was awakened by this nightmare. He had dreamt of this so many times.

Mitrajit felt sweat dripping from his head. He went out of the tent for some fresh air and washed his face. He looked around and could barely see in the darkness though there were some lanterns lit.

He took a few sips of water from the pot and came back into the tent to lie down on the mat. He could hear Chitraangad's snoring blended with other snores.

'I should have had another drink of Gaudi. It would have made me sleep well - or is it the two glasses of the drink actually messing up my sleep?' he wondered to himself before taking deep breaths.

Still unable to sleep, he tossed around, thinking of the various events that led to the Ustrakarnikas preparing to go to a war. They weren't even happening close to their region, nor did they have any direct relationship with the Kuru dynasty.

The past few years had been a concern for the Ustrakarnikas as they received the news of the continuous brawl between the Pandavas and Kauravas. Everyone in the Bharata varsha was on tenterhooks.

Aparajit would update them regularly about the animosity brewing between the cousins. Everyone was shocked when they heard the news that Duryodhana set up the Pandavas to live in the Lakshagriham[56] palace before ordering secretly to set it on fire. Everyone for almost a year thought that the Pandavas were dead.

It was a surprise when they came to know that the Pandavas were still alive and that they were in exile. This further increased the hate that Duryodhana had towards the Pandavas.

During the past decade, the Ustrakarnikas also saw an increased number of attacks by the Ekapaadas. The biggest challenge countering these attacks was that the Ekapaadas would not attack as a big army but always conducted melee attacks with smaller units. Their intentions seemed to be to loot the resources and demoralize the Ustrakarnikas.

There were many debates over how to thwart the Ekapaadas' attempts. Mitrajit brought up the idea that just as Krishna moved the Yadavas from Mathura to Dwarka to avoid the continuous attacks from Jarasandha, they should also move away from Devasthana after identifying a place somewhere north where they could be welcomed.

---

[56] Palace made from wax

Aparajit was not ready to accept this idea as he doubted they could get land somewhere else, as the Ustrakarnikas weren't as powerful as the Yadavas.

Some suggested attacking the Ekapaadas and destroying them so that they wouldn't dare to take on the Ustrakarnikas again. But the trouble with that was that the Ekapaadas were spread out far across the region between the Godavari and the Krishna rivers, and it would be difficult to take on them directly as it would take up lot of resources. Everyone agreed that it was better to defend themselves than go around pursuing the Ekapaadas on their ground.

During these uncertain times, one early morning the patrolling men spotted a group of Ekapaadas assembling on the southwest fence of Devasthana. They immediately alerted everyone in the village.

By the time Mitrajit came out of the house, he saw Chitraangad running towards him with Arochan and Subhadra. 'There are more than a hundred this time. Take our families along with rest of the women and kids and go to the hillock. I will go to the southern fence and try to stop them. Join me there,' he said.

Mitrajit took Purna, who was just a year-old baby at the time, in his hands, and along with Dhruti rushed to the hillock. Other women with their kids and elders followed them. Mitrajit left all of them on the hillock and told around twenty men to guard them.

He then went towards the fence to join the others in fighting the Ekapaadas. They fought for almost the entire morning before they could push the attackers back. The Ustrakarnikas lost almost seventy fighters, while they killed around eighty of their attackers. Though they had an upper hand, Aparajit was stunned with the number of losses on their side.

At the post battle assessment there was consensus that they should seek alliances with bigger kingdoms to keep the Ekapaadas at bay. Aparajit through his diplomatic relations connected with the Kalinga kingdom. He felt that they were the safe bet as the Kalingas were in close alliance with other regional sides like the Anga, the Pulinda and the Vanga. With Anga's King Karna being a close friend to Duryodhana, they thought it would also keep any invading tribes away from their region.

And it did work. For the next decade until now, there were no more incursions from the Ekapaadas. Having a strong ally helped the Ustrakarnikas. *But the same alliance brought us to this war,* Mitrajit thought. As he tossed and turned around in the bed to sleep, he recalled his father's advice. 'Good things happen to people who are patient enough.'

May be there could be some positive outcome out of this war. 'Hey Lord Shiva, please protect us,' he prayed silently as he dozed off into deep sleep.

5.Samudyama[57] Parva

Mitrajit was jolted from his sleep by Chitraangad. "It's time, Mitra. Looks like you are having trouble waking up early in the morning. Are you having nightmares again?' his friend inquired. Mitrajit was so tired and deep in sleep that he did not hear the sound from the conch announcing the beginning of the Brahma muhurta[58].

Mitrajit couldn't lie straight faced and nodded in agreement. 'After many days I dreamt about the day pitashri left us and I had trouble sleeping after that. My thoughts were wandering around after that until I fell asleep sometime in the late night. Sorry, that I had to tell you. My nightmares are nothing compared to yours.'

---

[57] Readiness

[58] Approximately 1.5hr before sunrise

Chitraangad put his hand on Mitrajit's shoulder and said, 'It is okay, Mitra. I know our parents are looking at us from above and wishing the best for us. Rest assured they can feel good that their kids are doing the right things for their family and for the tribe.'

Mitrajit smiled and got up to get ready. He saw that Arochan was up already, and others were getting ready. Everyone was preparing for the journey. After a few weeks at the training camp earlier, they all got used to waking up early before sunrise.

Mitrajit could sense that some men seemed more excited about participating in the war. *The youngsters, like Arochan, must be itching to showcase their skills and talents,* he thought. There was also anxiety among some, including himself, on how this war may end up.

Mitrajit and the other soldiers gathered their swords, shields and water bags. Aparajit joined them to check upon the shields and ensure everyone was ready and prepared for the journey.

"Now that calls for a pay raise," Chitraangad quietly said, winking at Mitrajit. Mitrajit looked at his friend to see what was on his mind this time.

"What? I am just saying that if our gear has the Kalinga's insignia that means we should be paid equally like the soldiers in their army and not just rely on our earnings on farming,' Chitraangad replied.

He has a point, Mitrajit thought. He looked at the insignia painted on his shield. The Shiva linga was shining bright in the middle of the shield. The Ustrakarnikas never had a special insignia. But with the new insignia, he felt that they were not some ancillary soldiers participating in the war but were officially part of the bigger alliance and would be fighting as part of an akshauhini.

Aparajit gathered every soldier from his tribe and gave an overview of the path that they were going to take on their way towards Kurukshetra. 'We are going to cross the kingdom of Nishada up north where the armies of King Hiranyadhanus will be joining us along. After that we will continue northward while staying close to the Yamuna River. We will be avoiding the Pandava's Indraprastha border before heading towards Hastinapura. We should be reaching Kurukshetra in the next two days,' he said.

Mitrajit and Chitraangad looked at each other. 'Are you thinking what I am thinking?' asked Mitrajit.

'If you are thinking about visiting the Nishada kingdom, then yes!' Chitraangad replied with excitement.

The Nishada kingdom under King Hiranyadhanus was a conglomerate of various tribes of bhils[59] on the north of Vindhyas. Mitrajit had heard valiant stories about how defiant they'd been over the years, defending against larger kingdoms. Their prince Ekalavya didn't agree to support Yudhishthira's Rajasuya Yagna[60].

Ekalavya had an acrimonious relationship with the Pandavas, as they were provided special attention by their teacher Dronacharya. Mitrajit and Chitraangad were surprised when they heard about how

---

[59] A tribe in central and mid-western ancient India. Mostly hunters and fishermen.

[60] Imperial sacrifice or royal inauguration sacrifice/consecration of king

Ekalavya, though he was a prince, was denied training under the Dronacharya's gurukul because he was a bhil and not a kshatriya[61]. They both felt that this was outright discrimination as they themselves were not kshatriyas but were capable enough to fight if needed.

Growing up, they always felt that someone's birth in a particular family or tribe should not be the reason to identify one as a great warrior. They appreciated the way Ekalavya taught himself the skills of archery all by himself while having a statue of Dronacharya for inspiration. They were also hurt and angry when they came to know that Ekalavya was asked to sacrifice his thumb as a fee by Dronacharya for using his statue as inspiration without his permission.

King Srutayush and other generals along with Aparajit were ahead of the rest of the units as most of them were on horses and they were followed by the Kalinga's cavalry unit. Ustrakarnikas, along with the Kalinga's infantry division, followed General Pattabhadra on foot.

The rest of the journey from the training camp to the Nishada kingdom was through a forest area. Mitrajit noticed that most of the pathway was already cleared for them, thanks to the elephant unit that went ahead of them. This made it easier to keep up the pace.

*****

---

[61] Warrior clan/background.

The past few days had been busy at Devasthana. With Kumudini organizing social gatherings to keep the villagers engaged, there was a sense of upliftment in the spirits of the people.

Purna was excited to participate in showcasing her khadga vidya. She was happy that there was an opportunity to impress her mother. Dhruti always encouraged Purna to learn swordsmanship as she herself didn't have a chance to learn when she was younger. 'I wish I could have learnt it earlier in my life; I would have been able to stop the attackers from killing pitashri,' she would always say to Mitrajit.

Subhadra, along with Dhruti, was excited to see Purna show her skills. The way she was handling the shield made Subhadra think of how Arochan would show his handling of the shield. He would take the shield from the back and immediately put it in front of face. 'Most of the opponents try to first hit on the head. So, it is better to put the shield in the front of the face as soon as you take it from the back amma,' he would explain.

Kumudini was happy to see Purna and other girls showcase their skills. 'The girls worked hard. Our men will definitely be surprised at the way our girls have taken up the khadga vidya. They can give a challenge to any one of them as they grow,' Kumudini said, sitting beside Dhruti and Subhadra.

'Yes, we can be assured that the future of Ustrakarnikas looks bright with the girls equally standing up to the boys,' Subhadra replied.

Purna walked over to Dhruti after her performance and was surprised with her mother's reaction. Dhruti hugged and kissed her on her forehead. Pitashri always did that, but now that he was not there it was nice to get the same response from her mother.

'You have done such a good job in learning and presenting your skills. Your pitashri will be proud of this performance,' a beaming Dhruti said to Purna.

'Arochan would be, too. I was amazed by the way you used the shield,' Subhadra chipped into the conversation.

'Thank you. Yes, braathaa taught me. I am glad you liked it too.'

On the next morning, Dhruti and Subhadra helped each other out with the harvest from their respective farms.

'We have to keep at least five to six bags of these vegetables in the barn under the hay for now. I doubt there will be any traders coming along this week,' Dhruti said.

'True. We will see what to do if they don't turn up next week too. We can't let the vegetables rot here,' Subhadra replied.

'Thanks to the war, everyone's lives have changed. Even the traders may be waiting for an outcome before they can think of which kingdoms to trade with. I hope the Kuru princes understand how their fighting has affected us all,' Dhruti said while moving her hand across her forehead, to sign that karma's written on the forehead, and this was all pre-determined.

'Well, I hope the right-side wins and ends all these troubles,' Subhadra replied.

93

'Which side is the right side, though? On one side, you have the Kauravas who were so keen in hanging on to their power that they wouldn't even hand over five villages to the Pandavas and tried to get them killed. On the other side, you have the Pandavas who continuously question Duryodhana's claim to the throne and are foolish enough to put everything at risk in a dice game they are so addicted to. And above all there is Krishna, who himself has avoided a war with Jarasandha and took his whole clan away to Dwarka but now is participating in a war between the Pandavas and Kauravas to confirm who takes the reins of the Kuru clan.' Dhruti said as her tone turned a bit emotional.

'All valid points, Dhruti. We will never know. But one thing is for sure: neither side is correct in getting their allies, relations, and friends across the Bharata varsha involved in this war along with their armies. Look at the amount of logistics needed to get this war going, and what about the aftereffects?' Subhadra replied.

'Absolutely! And what about the cost of this war? I am not even considering the financial cost, but the cost of lives,' Dhruti said, her tone breaking down further.

'Anyways let's not talk about this. The whole point of Kumudini's plan for these activities was for us to not dwell our minds on these discussions,' Subhadra replied to change the topic.

'True. Well, it was a good attempt for sure. Let us see how long this will help the villagers.'

*****

By evening, the whole contingent had reached the outskirts of Shrangverpur, the capital city of the Nishadas. King Srutayush and other generals were welcomed by King Hiranyadhanus and were staying in the king's guest house for the night while the army units settled down into the tents arranged for them.

'News is that the akshauhini of the Anga army will directly join at Kurukshetra. I have never seen such a gathering of armies, so I am also curious to see how it will look at Kurukshetra,' General Pattabhadra announced once they settled down.

'We are already surprised to see many units together both at the training camp and here. The thought of such a gathering alone excites me,' Chitraangad said.

'You look very eager, my friend,' Pattabhadra replied.

'Well, now that we are in this turmoil anyways, I better look forward to winning in this war,' Chitraangad replied as he twirled his long moustache.

'Of course, my friend. You have the right attitude. I hope everyone matches your attitude in the battlefield. Now, excuse me. I have to go and check on my troops.'

Once Pattabhadra left them, Chitraangad turned to Mitrajit and said, 'See? At least someone appreciates my attitude.'

Mitrajit laughed at his friend. 'Of course, Chitra. Now you need to rub it on to others.'

'Well, talking about positive attitude reminds me the morale of our men. It's been a few days that we have been out of Devasthana and some of them are concerned that we have no plans on how to keep the communication going between the villagers and us. I know it all happened quickly. I wanted to talk to Aparajit, but he is staying with the other generals in the king's guest house. Do you have any suggestions?'

'That is a good point, Chitra. It would be great to get updates from back home. Now that you ask me, I was thinking of making two groups with two of our men in each. The two groups may go to and fro, so that there is continuous and quicker information from either side. But with the distances, I don't know how feasible this is. Maybe General Pattabhadra can help with this. We could ask for four horses. This will allow the communication to be passed on much quicker.'

'Ah. I'd thought of sending a few men, but I like your idea of sending them in a staggered approach so that we can have updates from either side. As we move to the north, it will be difficult for us to get the information quickly. Let me check with Pattabhadra and see what his thoughts are. I will also talk to Aparajit in the morning. Thanks, Mitra,' Chitraangad said as he put is his hand Mitrajit's shoulder. 'I know I could count on you with a wiser suggestion.'

'I am always here to help out, Chitra. How is Arochan doing? I see he is pretty excited with the journey so far.'

'Well, he and his friends seem excited to see such large armies and we can only imagine how the youngsters must feel to be participating in this war with royals and princes they have only heard about in news. This is going to be their first big war. Even I get excited at the thought of being part of a large akshauhini. The biggest battle we would have had is the one almost a decade back with the Ekapaadas. And how many were involved in that? Maybe a few thousands between us and them. But look at this now. We are part of a full akshauhini and fighting in a land far away from our home. Who would have thought about this a few years ago?'

'True. I think just as we talk about the war in Lanka where many troops were gathered to fight with prabhu Ram, the future generations will talk about this war.'

'Yes, and I hope at least someone will recognize Ustrakarnika's participation in this war. Otherwise, the future will only know about the Kuru families and the kings who supported and nothing about the thousands of soldiers fighting under them in their Akshauhinis.' Chitraangad's face looked disappointed as he mentioned that.

Mitrajit put his hand on Chitraangad's shoulder and said, 'Let us not worry about that now, my friend. Let us be positive and hope that we all survive. I think that is more important for us than thinking of who will remember about us.'

'Makes sense, Mitra. You know I can get carried away very quickly. But you are right. Let us hope that we come out safely from this war.'

'Yes, my friend. Now let me go for my meditation.'

'Another important one of your routines. I am always surprised how consistent you are with your habits including meditating. Go ahead, Mitra.'

Mitrajit smiled and went to sit in the corner of the tent to meditate.

At dinner time, Mitrajit asked Pattabhadra, 'I really appreciate the way things were arranged at the training camp and here too. How do you plan for such camps? I cannot even think of planning for events in Devasthana, but this is huge.'

'The real reason is that we are trained for these kinds of arrangements, communication and adapting to changing scenarios in case of a war,' Pattabhadra replied. 'But of course, never on the scale of this one. This is new for us too. We've never had all our army units, cavalry, elephant, and infantry included, participate in a war. Usually, we would send a battalion or two but to gather the whole akshauhini only happened at military drill and never in a war. The only other time we have heard of this scale must be during King Ram's attack on Lanka.'

'Coming to the other reason,' Pattabhadra continued, 'it's the way our society works. We have specific people planning for these things in the administration whereas we have few generals whose focus is only on logistics. Most of us have our jobs streamlined and it creates expertise within those jobs. We have people who are just blacksmiths and others who are only farmers. I know it's different from your way of things, where most of you take up multiple jobs including farming your own lands and being trained warriors.'

'Absolutely. It's fascinating to see how each region and kingdom have taken up different routes to ensure their sustainability. One thing is for sure, the bigger the kingdom, the more resources they can allocate,' Mitrajit replied with a tone of appreciation.

That night, exhaustion from the journey helped Mitrajit to fall asleep early. When he woke up the next morning to the sound of the conch just before sunrise, he felt refreshed.

Before they were about to leave, Aparajit came to the camp. He took Mitrajit and Chitraangad to the side and asked, 'Hope everything was good last evening? I hope you both will understand that I must stay close with the commanders of the Kalinga as a sign of respect for them and our alliance. Let me know if our men are having any troubles and I will ensure we are catered for. Prince Sakradeva is very happy that we have kept our promise in supporting them and has promised to support us after this war to fight off the Ekapaadas once for all. He is also going to review the formation as he wants us to fight along with his troops as he appreciates our upper hand over others in swordsmanship.'

'Of course! The Pandavas and their allies will be done and dusted by the time they realize what hit them,' Chitraangad replied while twirling his moustache. Mitrajit thought he looked like his father, Rayvanth, whenever he twirled his moustache.

'Always ready you are, Chitra!' Aparajit replied with a smile. 'Now keep up the spirit and I will see you in the evening. As we are pacing up well, we may be camping near Indraprastha by evening. I will connect with you there again. May Lord Shiva bless us all.'

'There is one more thing before you leave. Can you check with the Kalinga generals if they can provide a few horses for us so that we can have communication between us and Devasthana regularly and quickly?' Chitraangad inquired with Aparajit.

'Oh sure. That is a good idea. I'll definitely check with them.'

'Thanks. It was Mitrajit's idea.'

'Not surprised. He always comes up with good suggestions,' Aparajit said while patting Mitrajit's shoulders. 'With you both beside me, I always feel supported. Now let me go and join the commanders.'

'So, Aparajit is now part of the biggies,' Chitraangad whispered to Mitrajit with a wink as Aparajit turned to go back to the Kalinga camp site.

'You better wait to say something after he leaves. You don't want to upset him now with your banter, Chitra,' Mitrajit replied.

Mitrajit knew his friend's intentions were never to insult but mostly to create a jovial environment, but he wanted to make sure Aparajit was also in the right mood. Not everyone was taking the news of the war calmly or looking forward to showcasing their fighting. He knew it wasn't easy for Aparajit to be relaxed.

He had the whole future of Ustrakarnikas in his hands. If the outcome of this war was positive for them, then with the support of Kalingas, the Ustrakarnikas would be able to look forward to a peaceful future. But if this war didn't end well, then history would remember him as the one who has entered the alliance with Kalingas, thus pulling them into this war.

'I understand Mitra. I just wanted to lighten it up for us. The old man knows me well. Anyways, let me go and get our men ready for the journey.'

The cooler temperatures that day helped the units to pace themselves faster than the previous day, and by afternoon they were able to reach the river Yamuna. The elephant units which were ahead of them were resting on the banks of the river.

The well armored elephants had huge mat-like hangings on either side with howdahs[62] on the backs of the elephants. These howdahs were big enough to hold two spearmen and two archers.

Looking at Mitrajit and Chitraangad, who were surprised to see such a huge unit of elephants, Pattabhadra said, 'It's time for them to rest. We don't want them to be tired. There are around twenty-two thousand of them in this unit.'

'No surprise the whole forest was trampled to make a clear pathway for us,' Chitraangad replied.

Arochan came towards them and said, 'Did you see those elephants? I never expected that I would see so many of them in my lifetime.'

All the Ustrakarnikas were in awe of the elephant unit. They had never seen so many of them together. It was a sight to behold.

After a quick break, the infantry started moving forward. The elephant units were getting ready too. Passing beside them, Mitrajit shivered at the thought of getting trampled by these elephants in the war. He looked at Chitraangad and before he could say something, his friend said, 'Just imagine fighting alongside these elephants in the

---

[62] a seat for riding on the back of an elephant or camel

101

war. Forget getting attacked by our enemies, we must be careful not to get stepped on by these beasts here.'

'Exactly my thoughts. It is amazing how these giants are trained and used in wars.' Mitrajit had studied about the use of elephants in war but never had an opportunity to see them in action.

As they were passing by the river Yamuna, Mitrajit noticed that the water in the river had a blueish color to it, unlike that of the river Godavari. He had never seen a river as wide as Yamuna. The waters flowed with vigor as if cleaning the land from its bad karma wherever it flowed. Looking at the river, Mitrajit wondered to himself why the plan was to go around the Yamuna River to reach Kurukshetra. It would be difficult to build bridges on the river, especially with the elephantry and cavalry units.

As they continued the journey northwards around the river, there were many towns and villages on their way. They could only see women and kids, and some elders, with most of the men from these villages having gone to join the other units for the war.

There was anxiety among the ranks as they closed in on the border of Indraprastha, the capital of the Pandavas. The cavalry and the commanders along with the royalty of the Kalinga were already camping at the border for the night.

Once they reached the camp, the Ustrakarnikas were greeted by Aparajit who was waiting for them. 'Welcome, my fellow people. I hope you came across the Kalinga's dreaded elephant unit as you passed by. Word has reached us that we will be joined by the

Narayani sena[63], who have been travelling from Dwarka in the west, in a few more ghadiyas. We should be reaching Kurukshetra tomorrow morning and wait for other army units to join. The Anga army will directly meet us at the camping grounds at Kurukshetra. Now take rest as today was a long day of walking. I will connect with Chitraangad and Mitrajit and they can debrief you all. See you in the morning.'

As the men were getting settled to rest for the night, Aparajit came to Chitraangad and Mitrajit. 'Hope things were good on the way here. I am sorry to say that the Kalingas didn't agree to provide us with any horses. They didn't want to divert their resources from the war. They did promise that their foot messengers would connect with our people at Devasthana on their way to Kalinga kingdom to inform them about our progress and that we'll be able get our updates once they are back. The only issue is that our people may get the updates delayed by few days,' Aparajit informed.

'Well, I didn't expect them to say no to our request,' Chitraangad replied immediately while snapping his fingers.

'As long as we're able to pass on our updates and receive news, we should be fine. That's all we want.,' Mitrajit replied.

'You are right, Mitra,' Aparajit said. 'But they are still going to get us our messages through their link of messengers all along the way.'

'Well, at least they have that option for us,' Chitraangad replied with a smirk on his face.

---

[63] army

'Yes, Chitra. In times like these, we have to take whatever is given to us. Anyways, I also have news that Kritavarma, the chief of Krishna's Narayani sena will be joining King Srutayush and other commanders today at dinner,' Aparajit continued. 'You may have an opportunity to connect with their generals. It is going to be interesting to see how this will unravel, especially with Krishna siding with Pandavas while his army is fighting alongside the Kauravas.'

'It was an interesting choice though. Who would say no to having a whole akshauhini unit supporting them? I think Duryodhana did the right thing in requesting the army. I know that Krishna is a very good strategist, and it will be a great morale booster to have him on your side, but he is not going to fight in this war as he promised. So what use is having such an accomplished warrior on your side only as a charioteer to Arjuna?' Chitraangad expressed what everyone was feeling but did not dare to question.

'True. It will be interesting to see how Commander Kritavarma and army will fight against Krishna and Arjuna if they come across each other in the battle,' Mitrajit chipped in, as he was curious about that too.

'Well, it will all unravel soon in a few days,' Aparajit said.

That evening before dinner, conches were blown to announce the arrival of Narayani sena. They were on a different side of the camp, so Mitrajit and company didn't get a chance to see them.

Mitrajit had trouble going to sleep that night as he was disturbed by the thunderous trumpeting sound from the Kalinga's elephant unit that also reached the campsite in the middle of the night.

Though they camped on the outskirts, the sounds were easily audible in the quiet, cold night.

*****

'So, acharya ji, can we predict who would win this war with the help of Jyotishya vidya[64]?' Purna inquired her teacher curiously.

'Why would you want to do that, Purna?'

'Well, I want to know if my pitashri along with other Ustrakarnikas will be safe and come home victorious.'

'Of course, you are curious about that. But I also want to ask you, do you want them to be safe or victorious or both?'

Purna took a few seconds to think and answered, 'I would want them to be safe but at the same time they are fighting a war, which means I also want them to be victorious. I am confused.'

'Of course, you are. For some winning the war is important and for some being safe is important. Imagine a king who lost most of his army but won the war versus a king who lost the war but was able to save most of his soldiers. Who do you think is the real winner? Let me ask you something. Who do you think won in the war between Ram and Ravana?'

'Of course, Sri[65] Ram won. He killed Ravana.'

---

[64] Astrological science

[65] Mark of respect like Sir.

'Got it. Now do you think Ravana's brother Vibhishana won in that war because he sided with Ram and was crowned the king of Lanka?'

'Yes,' Purna replied.

'Now think of this. What is the use of the throne if most of the army was killed, the kingdom got destroyed, and the world would see him as someone who betrayed his own brother?' acharya looked at Purna to see her reaction.

'Interesting. I never thought about it this way,' she replied.

'Absolutely. So, who has won depends on the perspective of who is writing history or whose side are you on. Some say that the Pandavas are fighting for dharma,' acharya continued, 'while others say Kauravas are fighting for what belongs to them. Now who is right, only the future generations can decide after weighing in all the reasonings from both the sides.'

Seeing Purna in deep thoughts, acharya said, 'Coming back to your question, one thing I can say even without looking into astrological signs is that the right side will win in this war.'

'That means our side will win. Ustrakarnikas are in the war for the sake of keeping our promise with our allies and to keep us safe from the Ekapaadas,' Purna replied.

'Every side thinks they are on the right side.'

When Dhruti saw Purna coming from gurukul, she could notice a disappointed look on her daughter's face. 'What is it dear? You look tired. Is everything okay?'

'I don't know amma. I am disappointed with acharya ji's reply. We had a good discussion on who is right and wrong in this war, but I am not fully satisfied with his answer.'

'Why? What did he say?'

'He refused my request to use Jyotishya vidya to check if we are going to win and if pitashri, Arochan braathaa and the rest will come home safely. He said that anyone on the righteous side will win. I know pitashri is on the righteous side so I have faith that he will be safe.'

'You are right, dear. We are fighting on the right side and we all can pray for Lord Shiva to keep us all safe. At the same time, acharya ji is right. Jyotishya vidya helps us understand many things but we don't want to have any hopes raised and I would agree that it should not be used to see if something works in the future.'

'I am not asking or praying for our side to win amma, though that would be good, all I want is to have them come back safely.'

Dhruti looked at her daughter and put her hand on Purna's head while moving her fingers through her hair. 'That is very thoughtful of you, Purna. You think the safety of our people is more important than just winning. I wish everyone thought the same way. We would not be in this situation if they did.'

She stopped for a second. She didn't want this discussion to be swayed again by her feelings. She immediately changed the topic.

JANYA BHARATA

'Anyway, I am planning to make your favorite yava[66] bread with lentils. Freshen up and come to help me. We will prepare together.'

The mention of her favorite bread brought a big smile on Purna's face. She looked up at her mother and said, 'If you think by changing the topic to my favorite dish I will stop thinking about the war, then you are wrong. But yes, let me freshen up and come to help you.'

Dhruti smiled at her and said, 'Clever girl! Just like your father. Never gives up. By the way, why don't you meditate too just like the way your father taught you? He will be happy to know that you were meditating.'

'Yes, I will do that amma,' Purna said as she rushed to freshen up. *Yes, I should be meditating*, she thought. *Pitashri will be so happy.* He used to teach her the techniques. He said it was his mother who taught him. He never said what happened to her, though. He did mention that his father was killed in an attack. *Maybe I should ask amma about this now that pitashri isn't here.*

'Amma, I am ready,' she said after freshening up.

'Good. Now mix this flour with water to make it into a nice dough. The bread will turn out smoother if the dough is done perfectly. Meanwhile let me light up the fire in the clay oven.'

As she started mixing, Purna asked. 'Amma, I have been wanting to ask pitashri this question, but he never gave me an opportunity. I have known a lot about grandfather, but we never speak much about grandmother. What happened to her?'

---

[66] Barley. Commonly used grain in ancient India around 6000BCE

Dhruti stopped for a second, surprised by that question arising out of blue. She took a long breath. *Maybe it is time that Purna should be aware of what happened,* she thought.

'Well, let me tell you. Don't forget to mix the dough though. After your grandfather was killed by the attackers, your father, his mother, me, Chitraangad and Subhadra reached Devasthana along with the dead body to complete the final rituals. It was an emotional time for all of us. We couldn't even enjoy our early days as newly married due to the death of your grandfather. Revati amma was obviously in shock,' Dhruti said.

'Now add some water to it to make it easier to mix. You can also add some oil to the dough as you mix to make it less sticky,'

Once Purna added the oil and continued making the dough, Dhruti continued, 'It was after a few days that she started acting a bit strange. She started putting the blame on me and the marriage. She said that I brought bad luck to the family and hence the events that unfolded. Your pitashri was shocked at this behavior because he highly respected his mother and was sad the incident influenced her behavior this way. She started ignoring me and even started shouting at me. Being young, it was hard for me. Luckily your pitashri supported me a lot. We both discussed and understood that the shocking news had affected her mental state.'

Purna continued to mix the dough, surprised to hear this story. She was also feeling sad on how it must have affected her mom. Her mom must have been only a few years older than what she herself was at this time.

'One evening, your pitashri confronted her and said it was inappropriate for her to think about me in the wrong way. She took time to understand that. I continued with the rest of the chores as diligently as possible trying to impress her. It took almost a year for her to realize that she was wrong in blaming me for all the events that unfolded with her husband. She felt bad about that and apologized for her behavior. But she kept on feeling guilty of her behavior. One day she took the decision to go to the forest and live the rest of her life alone as a sanyasi[67]. We tried our best to stop her and to tell her that she should live with us, but she was adamant.'

'Oh, so she is in the forest somewhere now?' Purna was curious to know where her grandmother was now that she heard about her story.

'Yeah. We don't know. She made us promise that we would not reach out to her and said that she wanted to leave this earth in peace when the right time comes. But one thing is sure, she was very nice to your pitashri, and he still appreciates all the things she taught him, including meditation. So, he will be very happy to see you practicing.'

'Definitely amma. I will practice.'

*****

---

[67] Renunciation

Next morning all the units started moving towards Hastinapura. The Ustrakarnikas and Kalingas moved together whereas the Narayani sena went ahead in front of them.

By mid-morning, clouds hovered above them and it started to drizzle, slowing down the pace of the units.

'Well, the rains can't dampen our spirits,' Chitraangad said. 'I will ask Maarthanda to sing for us.'

'That's a good choice. I always enjoy his singing,' Mitrajit replied.

Ustrakarnikas enjoyed the change of mood caused by Maarthanda's songs. The songs he chose were apt to the current weather and the situation they were all in.

Even after Maarthanda sang for everyone, Mitrajit was still thinking about the lyrics that were sung. There were a few sentences that really kept him thinking.

'You may look at the rain and say it's drenching and soaking you
or enjoy the refreshment it provides from the heat;
it all depends on the situation you are in,
but the rain still falls down no matter what you think about it.'

So true. We all may experience this war differently, but the outcomes will remain the same. One side will win and the other side will lose. But which side will win? Is winning more important than going home safely? Mitrajit's thoughts continued to bother him.

Looking at his friend's face, Chitraangad understood that his friend was still struggling with the thoughts of going to war. He took a deep breath and asked, 'What is it again, Mitra? We all know we are going to war and the reasons for why we are in this. Seeing you like this is bothering me and you know how cheerful I am to fight in this big war - even I am affected by your brooding.'

Mitrajit looked up to his friend and smiled. 'It is not that I am against it, Chitra. But just have a look around. An akshauhini of the Kalinga army with us and an akshauhini of the Narayani sena fighting against their own prince. What are we getting into? Imagine how many thousands of soldiers and war animals are being used in this war to douse the fires of a family feud. Is this all worth it? What would be the end outcome of this war? All we Ustrakarnikas wanted was to keep the Ekapaadas away from us, but the alliance has dragged us into this.'

Chitraangad was not surprised by his friend's response. He knew his friend is not someone who liked to fight or participate in battles, especially since his father's death. He has been noticing how this war had been tearing his friend apart internally.

'Well, Mitra, we just heard one of Maarthanda's songs. No matter what happens the rain will come down. It is our own perspective on how we see it. Similarly, the war is inevitable because several attempts at peace have failed. Yes, we've been dragged into this. But let's look at it like this. Either we can always be sad about why we were brought into this war or look forward to it and give our best fight to not only win but also to be safe.'

Mitrajit was amazed by Chitraangad's thoughtfulness. He felt foolish and selfish for thinking of only himself being dragged into this war. He took a deep breath and said, 'You are right, Chitra. I have been looking at this always from the perspective of why we were dragged into this war. But I think from now on I will focus on how to fight my best and go back home safely.'

Chitraangad smiled and said, 'That's the Mitrajit I was missing these past few days. One who thinks logically and not emotionally. Good to have you back, my friend. Now I know we can face any enemy and come back victorious.'

6.Purva⁶⁸ Yuddha⁶⁹ Parva

Just as they were closing in on Hastinapura in the afternoon, they saw a vast army unit on the west end. Word had reached that it was the akshauhini of the Chedi kingdom just down south of the Yamuna. They were on their way to join the Pandava group. The current king of the Chedis, Dhristaketu, was close to the Pandavas though his father Shishupala was slain by Krishna. *Interesting alliance,* Mitrajit thought.

Mitrajit, Chitraangad and Arochan were amazed at the sight of the vast armies marching ahead towards the north of Hastinapura.

---

⁶⁸ Before

⁶⁹ War

They hadn't seen such vast numbers of armies before. Though themselves were now part of an akshauhini, looking at one from a distance gave an idea of how large an akshauhini truly looked. The Chedi akshauhini covered almost 1-2 kos[70] area.

A few more hours of walking took them to the outskirts of the war zone: Kurukshetra, the land of the Kurus. Mitrajit got goosebumps as soon as he realized they were at the designated area. Mitrajit was expecting an open area between some hills, but this turned out to be a vast area of almost 20-24 kos with small hillocks in between. They had never come across a battlefield of such proportions. He felt anxious and excited.

General Pattabhadra informed them that they would be camping in the northeast zone of Kurukshetra. That's where most of the other Kaurava allied akshauhinis would be camping.

As they crossed the big area of empty land in the northeast direction, Mitrajit saw a huge army unit already camped close to their designated area.

'That is one akshauhini from the Trigarta kingdom,' Aparajit informed them. He had already reached Kurukshetra ahead of the other Ustrakarnikas and made the arrangements for them to camp. The Trigarta army, known as the Sampsaptakas, were famous for their bravery. They already fought a small battle with the Pandavas when the princes were on their exile at the Virata Kingdom.

---

[70] Unit of distance. Approximately 2 miles

115

Looking at the overwhelmed expressions on Mitrajit's and Chitraangad's faces, Aparajit responded. 'Yes, this is unusual for us. With the two akshauhinis of the Kalinga and Narayani sena along with the Trigarta army, the battle camp already looks so busy; imagine there are going to be a total of 18 akshauhinis by tomorrow evening with eleven of them fighting on Kauravas side and around seven on the Pandavas side. The whole battlefield will be filled with army units.'

'Speaking of the battlefield,' Aparajit continued. 'I have been informed that the muhurat[71] for the first battle is set for the sunrise in two days' time on the new moon day. So, get ready. You all have been walking for a few days now. It's time to have some rest before the battles. I will connect with you all tomorrow morning again to review the guidelines provided to us regarding the war, and to refresh ourselves on the vyuhas learnt at the training camp. Chitra, please inform the rest of our people.'

'Sure. I also have a question,' Chitra replied while looking at Mitrajit with a smirk. Mitrajit guessed from that expression that there was something funny coming up from his friend.

'Where is the actual battlefield? All I see is campsites and tents as if we are all here for a big luncheon,' he quipped.

There he goes, Mitrajit thought.

Aparajit looked amused at Chitraangad. He had known Chitraangad for many decades and knew that everything he said was

---

[71] Auspicious timing

in good humor. With a smile on his face he said, 'I wish that was the reason we are here. But our fate has brought us all here. Now rest up and I will connect with you all in the morning. You can reach out to me if you need anything or reach out to General Pattabhadra who is still your point person.'

Once everyone settled into their tents, Mitrajit went out for a walk around the campsite. He saw there were small hillocks around. He was curious to see how big the area was. As he was going towards the closest hillock, he saw Arochan talking to his friends. After realizing what Mitrajit was up to, Arochan inquired if he could join him too.

Both went up the hillock and looked around. There were tents as far as their view could reach. The war site must be spread across 4 to 5 yojanas, Mitrajit thought. Dust could be seen rising at a distance as more armies started reaching the battle zone.

'I never imagined this place to be so huge. All I see around is tents. There may be millions of men here all waiting to fight against each other.' Mitrajit said.

'Yes, me too - and actually, I am feeling a bit nervous, Taatsri[72],' Arochan said.

Mitrajit looked at the young man. He was staring off towards the campsites. 'What happened, son? I thought you were excited to take part in this war?'

---

[72] Uncle

'I was excited, Taatsri. I am still. It's just that I never thought this war was going to be at this scale. Look at all the army units, elephants, horses, and chariots. How are we going to fight against the maharathis, athirathis and rathis[73] in the war? We are trained well enough but still somewhere doubt creeps in my mind. I didn't want to express it to pitashri as you know how he may misunderstand my concerns. But you will understand.'

Mitrajit totally understood why Arochan was sharing with him. Whenever the young boy used to feel intimidated or pressured to do something, he would always seek his opinion.

'I get it, son. Let me tell you that at my age and even after experiencing so many battles, I too am feeling nervous about this war. I was doubtful as to why we're even fighting in this war. But the thought came that everything happens for a reason. We are here because of various reasons. We wanted to keep the Ekapaadas at bay and we wanted alliances to make us stronger. It is those alliances that brought us here. Maybe the universe wants us to participate in this war. We may end up on the winning side or on the losing side, only fate will decide. But one thing we can decide is how hard can we fight, not just to kill your enemies but to protect ourselves from being killed so that we can go back home safely.'

'But don't worry, just remove all the tension in your mind,' Mitrajit continued, 'and give it your best. It is through battles like these that young men like you can become tougher warriors.'

---

[73] Different military ranks based on the warrior's capacity to fight

Arochan looked at Mitrajit and said, 'Thank you, Taatsri. Those words do help me to calm my nerves. Again, as mentioned before, I am looking forward to this war and I look forward to going back home and telling stories about our successful fights with everyone.'

Mitrajit gave a smile and patted on the young man's shoulder. 'Let's pray that happens,' he said. He looked up as if to get assurance from the thathaastu devatas. 'Now let's go before everyone starts looking for us. It's almost dinner time.'

'Yes, and I know you may want some time for meditation before that.'

Mitrajit smiled and nodded. Both went back towards their tents.

Long lines of men were sitting in areas between the tents that were set for dinner. Large pots were brought in front of them which were tied to a long log held by two people. These large pots held variety of dishes for dinner. Each solider was served food in makeshift plates made from Palash[74] tree leaves.

'Elaborate and amazing arrangements,' Chitraangad said, sitting beside Mitrajit. 'It's like feeding the goat before killing it for its meat,' he whispered.

'Shh.' Mitrajit signed his friend to keep quiet while smiling at his joke.

At the dinner lines, Mitrajit saw that seated on the opposite side to them were soldiers from the Narayani sena, easily recognizable by

---

[74] A tropical tree like teak.

119

Urdhva Pundra[75] on their foreheads. They were seated tall and straight waiting to be served food.

'By the way, I got news from General Pattabhadra that though Kritavarma is taking command of the Narayani sena, another Yadava commander, Satyaki, is fighting on the Pandava side. It's like you and me fighting against each other,' Chitraangad said as he observed his friend watching the Narayani sena lines.

'Oh, is it? Now that just gets much more interesting. I am curious about the way the Yadavas have been participating in this war.'

As they were eating, Mitrajit felt some movement in the periphery of his vision. He looked to the left side of the line in front of him. He saw a person moving uncontrollably, seizure-like. Mitrajit noted the color of the person's face becoming paler. Everyone around looked at that person in shock.

'Put an iron chain in his hand,' some shouted, hinting that iron would help with the seizures. One of them was shaking him wildly as if to awaken him from sleep.

As everyone started surrounding the person, one young man shouted. 'Move aside. He is choking. Let me help him.'

Everyone moved aside. Mitrajit could now see the young man holding the struggling person and pushing hands into his chest. Within a few seconds, a big chunk of food came out of the person's mouth, and he took a long breath. He continued taking bouts of air and his face started coming back to normal color.

---

[75] A pattern with a vertical line between a U-shaped marking.

Everyone around was surprised with the sudden change in the scene. It took them a few seconds to realize what happened there. 'Glad we don't have casualties before the war itself,' someone from the group quipped.

Some of them clapped and few of them came to the young man and patted him. Mitrajit was also impressed by the immediate action of the young man. The young man looked to be in early twenties.

After dinner, as everyone started tidying up the place, Mitrajit went towards the young man.

'That was a quick move to save a life. I was amazed that you noticed and reacted so quickly,' Mitrajit mentioned appreciatively.

'Thank you. I am glad I was able to help,'

'How did you know he was choking?'

'My pitashri was a vaidya and I used to read books from his library. I read that when someone is choking, the airflow stops to the lungs and quick action needs to be taken to remove the choked food by pressing against the chest. Something I read when I was young. Glad it worked.'

'Impressive. Sorry for intruding. My name is Mitrajit, and I am from Devasthana. I am an Ustrakarnika. We are here as allies with the Kalinga army.' Mitrajit bowed with two hands as he introduced himself.

'No, no. Please don't do that. You are elder to me and a co-warrior. I should be bowing to you.' The young man bent forwards to bow in respect.

Mitrajit, who was already impressed by this young man's actions, was now overly pleased at his etiquette. He moved out of his bowing stance and gave a smile.

'Thank you. My name is Aayusha, and I am with the Narayani sena. We are here with our commander Kritavarma, and I report to General Satyavan.'

Just then, Chitraangad came with Arochan towards them.

'Here is my close friend, Chitraangad and his son, Arochan. This young man who just saved a person's life is Aayusha from the Narayani sena.' Mitrajit introduced each other.

They all bowed to greet each other.

'That was a quick response, Aayusha. Very impressive,' Chitraangad said.

'Thank you.'

As they were walking towards their respective tents, Mitrajit asked Aayusha. 'How is it like to be fighting with your army against your own prince?' The thought had been itching in his mind.

'Well, you know how it works with the royals and generals. They give orders and we follow. My role as a warrior is to give my best in the battlefield and survive while hoping to be on the winning side.' Aayusha sounded so clear in his thoughts.

'Agreed, Aayusha. Glad you have clarity at such a young age while we are just getting to understand the nature of this war. Well, it was nice meeting you. I hope our paths cross again.'

After coming back from the dinner, Mitrajit laid down on his bed and looked forward to a good night's rest after a restless previous night. *Two more nights of rest and then who knows what will happen*, he thought.

*****

Bhumi came running towards Purna and Suvarna. Seeing her friend panting and gasping for air, Purna was worried. 'What happened? Why such a rush?' she asked.

'I was on my way here when I saw the elder Mareechi talking to two men who didn't look traders. I think they were messengers. Let us go and know what message they may have from the battlefront,' Bhumi replied.

Purna got excited at that news. Finally, some updates. She ran towards the chatvaram, followed by Bhumi and Suvarna.

People were already gathered at the chatvaram. Everyone was eager to hear from the messengers who were talking to Kumudini and Mareechi.

Purna looked around for her mother. She wasn't there yet and neither was Subhadra. She then realized that both were harvesting today from Subhadra's farm as it was a clear day.

Everyone was looking and waiting eagerly for what the news was. There were lots of whispers and murmurs. Purna pushed through the crowd to go towards the messengers. She was just able to peek through the gap in the crowd. The guards' armors had shivalinga[76]

---

[76] Lord Shiva's symbol

insignias. *Possibly from the Kalingas,* Purna thought. They had to learn about various kingdoms and their flags in last year's classes.

Kumudini raised her hand as a sign for everyone to keep silent. She then stood up on the platform and announced, 'We have our friends from the Kalinga kingdom coming with the message. Looks like our men have crossed Hastinapura and are heading towards Kurukshetra. They may have reached by now. The war is being planned to start on the new moon day. We will have more information in a day or two as there are more messenger units coming in our direction as these two go back. I am sending message to our men that we are all doing good and pray for their successful participation in the war. May Lord Shiva protect them always.'

Purna ran towards Subhadra's farm. 'I need to tell my amma. I will meet you later', she said to her friends while trying to keep up the pace.

'Amma, there were messengers at the chatvaram. It seems pitashri and others have crossed Hastinapura and may already be at Kurukshetra by now. The war is going to start on the new moon day.'

Dhruti and Subhadra stopped cutting the crops and looked towards Purna.

'Only two more days for the war. Lord Shiva please protect our people,' Subhadra whispered.

'Thanks, Purna. I have kept your lunch in the kitchen. Have it before you go back to play with your friends,' Dhruti said.

'Okay, amma. I will play till evening and come back.'

'Not too late. Remember we are going to cook Pulasa fish today as we invited Kumudini for dinner.'

'Okay sure. I will come on time and help,' Purna ran back to play with her friends.

'There is something I wanted to ask you since yesterday,' Subhadra told Dhruti.

Dhruti looked towards her friend and asked, 'What is it?'

'A thought came to me yesterday. Now, don't get me wrong, but I was thinking that maybe we should be planning on what we could do if the results from the war are not in our favor?'

'You mean if something happens to our men, and they don't return.'

Subhadra nodded slowly, feeling embarrassed at even bringing up this question.

Dhruti took a deep breath and said, 'Well, I will be honest with you. I never thought about this, but I think it's a good thing to plan in case something happens. As I think about it, I am split between staying here and going back to Keertipuram. Both places are close to heart, though it's been decades since we went back to Keertipuram. The thought of passing through the Dandakaranya forest brings back the memories of that day of attack on Mitrajit's father. I don't know. I am confused.'

'Sorry to put you in this position. I am confused too. But I thought it would be a good idea as you never know what could happen.'

Dhruti nodded. Subhadra wasn't wrong, but Dhruti also didn't want to think about the repercussions of the war.

In the evening, Purna helped Dhruti prepare Pulasa fish for dinner. Purna felt the most daunting task was to remove the scales and wash the fish.

'Men appreciate when wives put in effort to make special dishes. Some dishes may look tough to prepare at first but once you know the proper way, it will be easier. Don't worry,' Dhruti explained.

Purna didn't take well to Dhruti's suggestion. 'Why should everything we do have to do with keeping the husband happy? I would like to learn how to cook this dish for myself. Even I want to enjoy some tasty dishes,' she replied in a disagreeing tone.

'Of course, dear. All I want is for you to be prepared for your future life, including married life. And I know you get upset with us discussing this, but you are at an age where we need to tell you these things. Otherwise, society will say that I was a bad parent who didn't teach her daughter well.'

'I am not interested in what society will say, amma. If society had cared for us, they would not have called for an unwanted war that could have been solved by diplomacy or only involved the fighting Pandavas and Kauravas. Why bring everyone else in the Bharata varsha into the dispute?'

Dhruti was surprised at Purna's response. Poor child is so affected by the war that she is taking out her frustrations through different ways, she thought.

'Okay now, cool down. Let's not again talk about the whys and why nots of the war. Let us concentrate on cooking. You need to put one small cup of salt and pepper for this amount of dish,' Dhruti continued the recipe to change the topic.

Mother is correct, Purna thought. *There is no use of bringing up the need of the war again and again.* Once the river water flows down into the salted sea, there is no way to bring the fresh water back into the river. With a deep breath, Purna followed her mother's instructions and added the spices to the dish.

*****

After a good night's sleep, Mitrajit woke up feeling fresher than previous days. Camping in the forest wasn't comfortable with the bedding pressing against many sprawling roots on the ground.

He stretched and walked towards the washroom area set up over the other side of the campground. Such a well thought arrangement with small pop-up sheds to provide privacy for the soldiers, he thought.

After freshening up, he went towards the small hillock where he had gone the previous evening with Arochan. He gazed at the sun as it started to come up at the horizon. The view was clear in the early morning. It wasn't like the previous evening with all the dust rising in the sky from the arrival of the soldiers.

How long will this clear sky last? he thought. Tomorrow once the war starts, it will be nothing but dust and vultures looking for dead bodies. Mitrajit's thoughts slowly moved away from the tents and took him to Devasthana.

He would wake up Purna and Dhruti early on days like this with clear skies to watch the sunrise. They would go to the small hill behind their home. On some days, the early morning fog would cover the valley and create a beautiful scene with the sun's rays punching through the fog, trying to reach the plants and ground below.

'Ah, there you are. Dreaming about being with Purna and Dhruti, and watching the sunrise?' Chitraangad's voice brought Mitrajit from his thoughts.

Mitrajit smiled. He wondered how his friend knew his thought process so easily. 'Was it so obvious?' he asked.

'Of course, Mitra. You are bad at acting for sure. It's an amazing view from here, though. Look at all the armies. More joining by today. Millions of soldiers. Anyways, let's go as Aparajit would like to meet us all to review and discuss strategies for tomorrow.'

As they were going down the hill towards their camp, Mitrajit said, 'There is one thing I wanted to talk to you about. It's about Arochan.'

Chitraangad looked toward his friend in curiosity. 'What happened?'

'He was feeling a bit overwhelmed with the thought of participating in this war and feels that you may misunderstand him if he tells you that. He feels you may think he is afraid. He is not afraid, but just feeling a bit nervous.'

'Of course, I understand. If we are feeling edgy with the things going on around us, I can only imagine what is going on in his mind. Glad he could come to you and express his concerns. But hope he is feeling ready to fight?'

'He is, Chitra. Don't worry about that much. I just wanted to give you a heads up.'

'Thanks, Mitra. With you on my side, I can be assured that we will both keep him safe. No matter what happens to me, my hope is that he will go back to Devasthana safe and sound.'

'Mark my word. I will ensure no harm comes to him. We should fight closer to him and keep an eye on his safety.'

As Chitraangad and Mitrajit came towards the campsite, they saw Aparajit was waiting for them.

'Ah. There you are. Let us get started with the briefing.'

Chitraangad summoned all the Ustrakarnikas together. Aparajit stood on a platform and was holding a few documents.

'Hail Lord Shiva. My dear Ustrakarnikas, hope you all had a good rest. There are a few highlights and updates I would like to bring to your attention before tomorrow's battle.'

Everyone around him became quieter. Each one of them was curious to know how the next day would unravel for them.

'First of all, his highness the elderly Bhishma will be commanding our forces. He will be in constant touch with King Srutayush, through whom I will get our orders. One other update is that though the Anga army will be fighting in this war, King Karna will not be joining the war due to some disagreements with Bhishma.'

There were murmurs around the crowd at that news.

'It is getting ridiculous. Firstly, we have Krishna, whose army will be fighting against him and now we have Karna whose army will be fighting but not him. And we are dragged into this war. The royals have their own ways and wishes,' Chitraangad whispered slowly under his breath so that only Mitrajit could hear.

Aparajit looked sternly towards Chitraangad. He was close enough to hear the whisper. Chitraangad understood that it was the wrong time to say anything and bowed his head down.

'We will be taking a Sarvatomukhi Danda[77] formation while facing west and southwest,' Aparajit continued. 'Our group, along with some battalions of the Narayani sena, will be following the Kalinga cavalry on the far north side. We must be quick to follow up behind the steeds and support the cavalry. Remember that we will be following all formations and strategies of the war that we talked about at the training camp. At the same time, we are also given some rules for this war framed by Bhishma, agreed upon by both sides. These rules are an attempt to reduce deceit, save lives and participate in a dharma yuddha[78].'

Aparajit took a document and started announcing the rules.

'Fighting must begin at sunrise and end at sunset.

---

[77] Formation where best commanders will form a circle supported by flanks on either side.

[78] Ethical war. War fought with righteousness.

A single warrior should not be attacked by multiple warriors at the same time.

Only warriors with similar weapons can duel.

Surrendered warriors should not be killed and will be subject to protection as a prisoner of war.

No one will attack an unarmed or unconscious warrior.

No one will attack a warrior from the back.

No one will strike an animal which is not a direct threat.

Warriors will fight their equals according to the titles given to them. For example, a maharathi will only fight with one with that title.'

Aparajit took a break from his announcement. He looked around to get a gauge of the reactions from his fellow Ustrakarnikas.

'Take your time to go through these rules again as we need to make sure we follow them. Personally, I think these rules will make it much easier for us to participate in this war and be as safe as possible. Do reach out to me if you have any questions by afternoon and I will be able to get more information needed from various commanders of Kalinga,' Aparajit ended his announcement.

Aparajit came down the platform and signaled Mitrajit and Chitraangad to come to one side.

'Do you have any doubts on the rules?' he inquired.

'Well, to be frank, I am still trying to comprehend all of these rules,' Chitraangad said.

'These are definitely a good on paper and it will be great if everyone follows them,' Mitrajit replied. 'But I don't know how much to trust these rules. We may follow them but if the attackers don't follow the same, I don't know how it will be safe for us. I am also confused how we will take into consideration the arrows shot by archers or if the elephants go berserk.'

'Exactly my thoughts too,' Chitraangad chipped in.

'Well, I also have similar doubts. But I am here to let you know the rules that were drawn by higher ups. I think every commander and general hopes that both sides will respect these rules. And let us hope that these rules will help us fight this war with goodwill and at least give us an even chance.'

'True. Let us hope for the same,' Mitrajit replied. He took a second and continued. 'Don't mind asking you this but I hope you are doing fine too with all these fast-paced changes. It must be hard for you to keep up with the information and decisions regarding the war.'

'Thanks for asking, Mitra. These are the perks of leadership, for good or bad. Our people look upon us to guide them and make decisions that will help all of us. One day, you both will have to make decisions that may be difficult for you, but you need to take into consideration what will be the best for our tribe. Just as I took the decision of joining with the Kalingas. I know that this was the best option we had. Now let us get back to our units and be available for any questions they may have. Let us show them that we are here to support them all through this process.'

*****

In the afternoon, after lunch, Chitraangad came to talk to Mitrajit. 'There is an urgent issue. We need to get to Aparajit urgently,' he said.

'What happened?'

'Viraata wants to leave us and go back to Devasthana. He doesn't want to participate in this war anymore. I tried to talk sense to him, but he is not ready to budge. I am afraid he is influencing others too to leave and go back. We need to get Aparajit to talk to him.'

'Really! What made him think so?' Mitrajit was surprised to hear the news.

'Let's go and I will explain on the way.'

As they were heading towards Aparajit's tent, Chitraangad said, 'Looks like Viraata got cold feet. He said that he understands the need of the alliance and supporting our allies because of that. He was fine all these days, but I think today's rules made him doubt. He doubts the opponent troops will follow these rules even if we follow them. He wants to go back to Devasthana. He is also creating a ruckus making everyone around him also start doubting the rules.'

'No surprise he has doubts about everyone else following the rules. But I think it's too late now to get out of this. He needs to understand that we need to see the bigger picture here,' Mitrajit replied.

'Exactly my thoughts. But maybe Aparajit can help him understand.'

Aparajit was shocked to hear the update. 'If he had doubts, he could have approached me when I announced the rules. And these

133

rules are actually in place to safeguard and equalize the playing field. Let's go and connect with him before he starts influencing others.'

Aparajit along with Chitraangad and Mitrajit came to the Ustrakarnika camp site to find Viraata packing up and talking to a few others in the group.

'Ah, there you are, Viraata. I heard from Chitraangad that you wanted to leave to go back to Devasthana as you don't feel the rules will be followed,' Aparajit asked.

Everyone else including Viraata stood up and looked at Aparajit. There was a feeling of guilt in their faces and Viraata looked down to the ground.

'I am sorry that I have to say this, Aparajit,' Viraata said as he continued to look down. 'But I feel that the rules will not be followed. I don't want to risk my life. How can it be confirmed that nobody will hit me from the back, or no one will try to hurt me when I keep my weapons down to take a break from the fighting? I have doubts about these rules and so do some of our men.'

'I can understand your concerns, Viraata, because these are exactly what I have been thinking too,' Aparajit replied.

Everyone looked at Aparajit, surprised at his response. It was surprising to hear that even their leader felt the same.

'These are not the rules we are used to, nor that we think everyone will absolutely follow in this war, but it will give us some confidence to fight in this war with the many soldiers who are trained just for that. These rules will make it at least a fair ground to start from. It will give us an opportunity to give a good fight. And that is what I am asking you all. Let us give our best at this fight,' Aparajit said.

'But it's not our fight,' Viraata replied, this time looking into Aparajit's eyes. 'We didn't sign up to be allies of Kalinga to fight this war but to have their support in our battles with the Ekapaadas. Now we are dragged into this unnecessary war that is not ours. I am fine as long as its Kalinga's war, but this is not even their war either. Why are we doing this, then?'

'How can you say this is not our war? This is our war. Kalingas have been on our side all these years and it is time for us to be on their side. Is it directly our war? Nope. But is this our war? Yes. When we win this war, it is going to send a huge message to the Ekapaadas that we are never to be messed up with. But if we leave this war, they will see us as weaklings. That will embolden them to attack us further. We don't want that. So, either we fight this war with whatever rules they have come up with to give our future generations a sense of peace and safety, or we don't fight this war and put them at risk,' Aparajit replied with a stern tone.

Everyone in the tent silently listened to Aparajit. They had rarely seen him raise his voice this way.

'Look around this campsite. Millions of men from far regions have come to participate in this war. Why do you think they are all here? Because we all follow our dharma, which says never to back away from your promise and to stand by with your friends in times of need. Our friends need our support. Our future generations need safety. We cannot run away from our dharma. If you still think you want to go back, you are more than welcome to do so, but please decide quickly. Either you stay and give your best fight, or you leave immediately without affecting everyone's morale. May Lord Shiva guide you towards the best decision.'

Aparajit took a pause and looked at Chitraangad and Mitrajit. Both gave a small nod to show their agreement with him. With that, Aparajit left the tent. Chitraangad followed him.

Mitrajit went to Viraata and put his hand around his shoulder and said, 'Hear me out, my friend. Just as Aparajit said, I totally stand by your feelings. We all are overwhelmed by the situation we are in. Look at me. I am here leaving my kid and wife too, but with the hope that once this war is done and with Kalingas on our side the Ekapaadas will not dare to attack us again. Also, Aparajit has been lobbying to get support from the Kalingas to close the feud with the Ekapaadas once and for all once this war ends.'

Viraata looked into the eyes of Mitrajit. 'Thanks for understanding my troubles, Mitra. I know that I am not the only one feeling this way. But I also agree with what all you and what all Aparajit have said. I need some time to think through this. You know it's not easy.'

'Of course, Viraata. Let me leave you to that. But I hope we all fight together in this war. I will see you in the evening.'

Chitraangad met Mitrajit outside the tent. 'I knew he would prefer to listen to you than to me. I wanted to just hit him to get his wisdom back into his brain.'

Mitrajit smiled, 'Thank God, it was me then. Let's hope that he changes his mind.'

In the evening as everyone was heading for dinner, Viraata approached Mitrajit. 'Thank you for talking to me earlier Mitra. I gave a thought to everything Aparajit and you said, and I have decided to stay put. He was right. The rules are there to make it easier for warriors like us to fight in this war. If we fight our best, we may be safe and be victorious. Please count me in. I am also feeling a bit awkward to talk to Aparajit after the commotion I created. Thought maybe you could pass on this message to him,' Viraata said.

Mitrajit gave a hug to Viraata and said, 'Good to know, my friend. Everyone in this war is here for a reason and I know our need will prevail and we will be victorious. Let us go to Aparajit. Let me tell him the good news. He will be thrilled.'

'You want me to come with you to be in front of him after all that?' Viraata was hesitating to show his face to his leader after the afternoon's experience.

'Of course. He is our leader, and he is very understanding. He will be happy to see you rather than just getting the message. Now let us go.'

After hearing from Mitrajit about Viraata's change of mind, Aparajit gave a smile. He got from his chair and went close to Viraata and gave him a hug.

'May Lord Shiva bless you. I know it was a difficult decision, but I am glad you made the right decision. Together we will conquer the

Pandavas and their allies and then we will conquer the Ekapaadas,' Aparajit said.

'Now that we are all back at the saddle, let us enjoy our big dinner before the main event tomorrow,' Chitraangad chirped in.

Everyone clapped and laughed. *What better way to end this day? Never mind what tomorrow will bring*, Mitrajit thought.

7.Yuddha[79] Parva

This is it, Mitrajit thought as he got up from the bed. He came out of the tent, seeing the sky on the eastern horizon turning into an orange tone. It was almost time for sunrise. Mitrajit's hands immediately came together to bow towards the sky.

'Lord Shiva, please keep us and our families safe.' He took a pause and then continued praying 'Lord Shiva, apologies for being selfish. Keep everyone safe. I also hope you can understand that I have to take lives today as part of my role and as self-defense. Please forgive me.'

---

[79] War

The whole camp site was abuzz with sounds of weapons, animals and men squandering around as everyone got ready to be in positions.

Aparajit came towards the Ustrakarnikas and said, 'May Lord Shiva protect us all and let us give a good fight in this war. This is going to be an unprecedented war with around five million warriors and as many elephants and horses present at this ground to fight for what is due on this earth - peace. Remember the rules and take advantage of them to take rest while possible. We will be supported at the front by the archers, and we will follow up behind Kalinga's cavalry. We will fight alongside the dreaded Narayani sena, so we have nothing else to fear. I will be passing on any orders to you as I get them from Prince Sakradeva and other Kalinga commanders. Let us show the Pandavas and Kauravas along with their allies what Ustrakarnikas are made of and the grit we bring to this war. See you later in the evening on the victorious side. Hail Lord Shiva.'

Everyone in the unit shouted, 'Hail Lord Shiva.' With that they all started taking positions as the light from the horizon started brightening up the skies.

There were thousands of army units taking up positions along the vast Kurukshetra ground. The Ustrakarnikas walked up to the north side to stand behind the Kalinga cavalry.

General Pattabhadra came towards Chitraangad and Mitrajit. 'Nice to see you both, my friends. I will be on the western flank with my soldiers. I see that you are on the eastern flank along with the

Narayani sena. I wish you all the best and will see you on the other side of victory,' he said as he left towards his unit.

Aparajit gathered everyone in three groups with each group headed by one of the experienced warriors including himself heading one of the groups. Chitraangad's group included Arochan while the last group was headed by Mitrajit along with Viraata and Maarthanda.

Viraata came up to Mitrajit and said, 'Thank you for bringing back confidence to me and having faith in me. I will not let you down.'

Mitrajit smiled and replied, 'Don't thank me, my friend. We all are fighting for the future of Ustrakarnikas. We are fighting for our families, and we are fighting for our friends at Kalinga. Let us not let them down. Let us give our best.'

Viraata nodded in agreement.

Mitrajit noticed that to the right of their group was the Narayani sena. He could barely recognize Aayusha in that unit, because of the head gear he was wearing. It could be him, he thought when he saw a young face under that head gear. He turned towards his left and saw Chitraangad looking at him. They both gave a smile to each other.

'It is nice to see Arochan in your group. Let us keep him as close to us as possible,' Mitrajit said. Chitraangad nodded.

'Can't see anything ahead because of these horses and the archers in the front. No idea what is going on the other side,' Chitraangad said.

'True. No idea if we will see those chariot riding warriors from either side,' Mitrajit replied.

'Well, I want to see them but definitely do not want to encounter them.'

Both had a good laugh at that. They looked towards Arochan and saw the young man looked concentrated and in the zone.

'Stay with us, Arochan. Don't stray too far from us,' Chitraangad told him.

'Okay, pitashri,' he replied. He then looked towards Mitrajit and nodded in acknowledgement.

At that moment, the whole ground suddenly lit up bright. The light from the rising sun reflected on the chariots, shields and swords, and lit up the sky. The commencement of the battles would be announced any time now, Mitrajit thought.

Aparajit was talking to other generals in front of him from the Kalinga army. He looked back to others and said, 'The Pandavas have taken Vajra[80] formation. We are waiting for Bhishma and others to blow their conches anytime to announce the start of the war. They also have got news that prince Yuyutsu, the maharathi and the stepbrother of Duryodhana, has decided to fight for the Pandavas. He has moved towards the other side along with a few troops.'

Aparajit had to shout on top of his voice to convey that message as the sounds from the huge army units were noisy and continuous.

---

[80] Diamond

'Well, more war drama, eh?' Chitraangad said to Mitrajit while looking back to ensure Viraata didn't hear him. 'First it was Karna not fighting, and now a change of sides for the prince. Who knows what we'll hear in the next few days.'

As Mitrajit was about to reply, he was disturbed by a sudden bustle among the troops. He looked towards the front, trying to get a view of what was happening while dodging the horses in front of him. All he could see was a plume of dust rising from the ground as the sound of a chariot moved across the battlefield.

Aparajit shouted, 'Looks like Arjuna's chariot with Krishna as his charioteer. It seems he is taking a final assessment of the Kauravas formation before the start. No idea what they had in mind.'

After a few minutes, they got news that Arjuna had dropped his weapons down and Krishna was talking to him.

Not surprising that even a great warrior and prince like Arjuna who was considered one of the main warriors in the Pandava side also got cold feet. Who would not? Mitrajit thought. Viraata was at least expressive, while Mitrajit himself was having doubts about participating in this war.

We are fighting the unknown enemy in this war, Mitrajit's thoughts continued, but imagine fighting against your teachers, cousins, and relatives. That's what must have gotten Arjuna worried just before the battle. Though he had the great strategist in Krishna and all other warriors supporting him, he still had to fight against his own teacher, Dronacharya, and against his grandfather, Bhishma, who was commanding the Kaurava side.

Everyone started to become restless with the wait.

'No idea how long the discussion will go on. We were told that the battle would start at sunrise but here we are a few minutes after sunrise and still no sign of any start time,' Chitraangad said as he was getting restless himself too.

The horses in the cavalry in the front started moving around as they could not stand still for such a long time.

After a few more minutes, word came from the frontlines that Arjuna and Krishna were now heading back to their troops. What has happened now? Probably Krishna would have talked Arjuna into taking up the weapons again and getting ready for the fight. Kings and royals have their way. What if I didn't want to fight a war right now? Could I drop the weapons and go back? He didn't want to think about these questions as he had already made up his mind to fight in this war.

Just then, the sounds of conches became louder and clearer. All the generals within each flank of the army started blowing their conches. Mitrajit guessed they'd have gotten their permissions to attack from the Commander in Chief Bhishma.

Chitraangad gave a look at Arochan and Mitrajit before turning towards Aparajit. They all made quick eye contact with each other and nodded in acknowledgement. They all knew it was time, finally.

Mitrajit tightened his grip around the sword. He took the shield from his back and held it in front. It may be a few minutes before he would be in a fight, but it was better to be prepared for the arrows first. You never know which direction they will fly in from and how deep into the units they'd reach.

The cavalry in front of them started moving ahead and they all started running behind the horses. Just then, the sky started to get darker.

'Arrows incoming,' someone shouted. Mitrajit looked up and saw a barrage of arrows coming in their direction while some of them fell in front on the cavalry.

He immediately took hold of the shield and braced for the impact. Lots of arrows came flying their way and the force with which they were hitting the shield was making it difficult for Mitrajit to hold it steady. A few of the arrows were piercing the shield, but not enough to cut through it.

Everyone was trying their best to hold off the arrows even as they continued to rain on them. Mitrajit could hear the cries of pain all around him. Mitrajit looked around while shielding from the arrows and saw some of the soldiers in his group were hit by the arrows, blood gushing out of them.

It was so different when they were fighting with the Ekapaadas. It was a direct attack by swords, and it was more about dodging the swings from the swords. Here it's about dodging the arrows even before the actual one on one battle starts, Mitrajit thought.

Whenever the arrows stopped falling on them, the units would take few steps to move forward. Mitrajit noticed some soldiers were already dead on the ground. It was becoming difficult to move forward while stepping over these dead bodies, and while their vision was blocked by the shields. Slowly and steadily Mitrajit moved ahead, followed by his unit.

After a few minutes, the rain of arrows stopped. With that, Mitrajit noticed a huge gap between them and the cavalry in front of them. The cavalry galloped ahead onto the opposite side as they raised a layer of dust behind them.

Realizing the Kaurava infantry may start coming towards them anytime, Aparajit shouted, 'Everybody get ready. Anytime now.'

Mitrajit looked around. Everyone started running towards the opposite side. Through the dust in front of them, he could see soldiers running towards them. Mitrajit and others started moving forward while avoiding the injured bodies already spread along the ground. There were horses running astray after their riders were killed. It looked chaotic for a few seconds.

Mitrajit saw a soldier running towards him. In his periphery he could see that the Narayani sena was already ahead on his right side and engaged in the fighting.

As soon as the soldier came within arm's reach, Mitrajit bent his body and swung his sword hard. The soldier was surprised with the sudden move by Mitrajit and even before he could bring his shield down or jump over the sword, the sword went through his legs. Mitrajit could feel the sword being stopped for a second by the bone and then cutting through it and coming out of the leg. The soldier fell onto his face. Just before he was about to hit the ground, Mitrajit hit his head with the shield. The soldier fell with a thud and didn't get up again.

Mitrajit felt a burst of confidence. He rushed forward with adrenaline pumping in his blood.

Mitrajit noticed that most of the soldiers they were fighting against were fair skinned. Looking at the insignia on their shield, he confirmed them to be the Kekeyas from the northwestern frontiers of the land.

Mitrajit went on to fight another soldier who rushed towards him. A fierce exchange of blows ensued. Just then, a horse came running wild towards them without a rider. The Kekeya soldier moved slightly to his left to avoid being hit by the horse. Taking this as an opportunity, Mitrajit stabbed the soldier on his neck while he was trying to swirl around. Blood oozed out immediately and he fell. For a second Mitrajit felt if he did the right thing by attacking the soldier as he moved aside. But he realized it could have been himself in the soldier's place if he didn't attack.

Nevertheless, Mitrajit continued. He could get a glimpse of Arochan fighting few meters from him along with Viraata on the other end. Mitrajit tried to make sure he was as close to Arochan as possible so that he could support him if needed.

*****

For the next two ghadiyas there was no opportunity to take rest; the attacks were relentless and nonstop.

Mitrajit started to feel fatigued with the continuous fight. He needed to stop but was worried if the opposite soldier would hit him if he kneeled to take rest. He shouted to Viraata. 'I am going to take a break. Cover me if needed.'

With that, he took a few steps backwards and put his sword and shield down before kneeling to take a breath. He noticed that there was a soldier who was rushing towards him but stopped after seeing him keeling and then went in a different direction. Phew, they do follow the rules, Mitrajit thought.

He took a cloth and wiped the sweat off his forehead. With sweat came off the blood drops on his forehead that must have been from the soldiers he fought. He didn't care. There was already so much blood on him that others may think he was injured.

He saw Chitraangad fighting at a distance from him. He turned to his left to see Arochan taking a break too.

While looking towards Arochan, Mitrajit took a small sip of water from the leather pouch hanging around his waist. The cold water that he filled up the pouch with was almost warm by this time. A few sips made him feel better.

Mitrajit saw Aparajit and Viraata fending off their respective opponents. Aparajit is quick for his age, he thought. On the right, he saw Aayusha fighting with a sword and a spear. He looked ambidextrous and was wielding his spear so well that no one would dare to be in the close radius around him.

Mitrajit looked around. There were so many dead bodies around him and many more injured. The injured soldiers were either screaming in pain or watching the ongoing battles while waiting for the medics to come and pick them up. He saw that some of the 'lucky' ones were being picked up by the medic chariots, which could be identified with a green flag with a fire symbol, taking them back to the camps.

At least fifteen so far either killed or injured by him, Mitrajit thought as he was looking around. Counting will not help, especially with so many millions of soldiers participating. He himself alone might have to take on hundreds of them by the time this war ended, or he himself might end up being one of them.

After that short break, Mitrajit put the leather pouch around his waist and got up. Taking up the sword and shield, he looked around. He saw another Kekeya soldier running towards him. It never ends, he thought as he tightened the grip around the shield and wielded the sword to block the attack by the Kekeya soldier.

Expecting Mitrajit to block his attack with the shield, the Kekeya soldier looked perplexed for a second and then noticed that Mitrajit was using his shield to hit him. Mitrajit went hard at the soldier's head with the shield and knocked off his helmet. The soldier fell like a log.

One more to the dust, Mitrajit thought. He continued moving forward, attacking, and defending. For the next four hours, the battle continued. Though the Kaurava allies had upper hand they couldn't gain momentum yet.

Mitrajit took breaks when needed as he felt tired by afternoon. He was indeed becoming older but at the same time, never had fought such long battles. The longest he'd fought was for 3 to 4 hours when the Ekapaadas attacked them almost a decade ago.

Mitrajit continued with his technique of keeping the element of surprise while fighting the Kekeya soldiers. From bending and turning around his direction to engaging his sword as defense and his shield to attack, he continued fighting hard as the afternoon sun continued shining onto the ground below.

As another soldier rushed towards him, Mitrajit suddenly felt a sharp pain in his right shoulder. A stray arrow came towards him and hit his right shoulder. It went straight in. For a second, Mitrajit was agonized by the pain, but seeing the soldier rush towards him, he blocked the attack with his shield. For a few seconds, Mitrajit couldn't move his shoulder. The pain was overtaking his need to fight.

After blocking three more swings from the opponent's sword, Mitrajit bent and kicked on the knee of the opponent soldier. The soldier, not expecting this, lost his balance. Taking the opportunity, Mitrajit hit him with the shield and kicked him in the face. The soldier fell down unconscious.

With the piercing pain he was experiencing, Mitrajit dropped his sword and shield down on the ground and kneeled. He looked at the arrow and it was not as deep as it felt, but the pain was excruciating. It must have hurt a sensitive nerve, he thought.

Without further delay, while holding the arrow with his left hand, he pulled it as hard as he could. The arrow came out with some blood and for a second the pain was unbearable. He saw that there wasn't much blood coming out which he took as a good sign. He took the cloth he used to wipe his forehead and put it on his right shoulder and gave it a press.

He then slowly tried to raise his shoulder. It was hurting but at least he could move it a bit. He continued moving his arm till he felt good about it. He thought of taking a break from the battle and going back to the camp but then he saw Arochan fighting hard and looking to be struggling. Not seeing Chitraangad around, he took up the sword and moved towards Arochan.

Arochan was able to fend off the soldier's attack by fighting valiantly and killed him by slicing his torso. He felt tired after that long fight and knelt below to take a break.

As Mitrajit was approaching Arochan's side, he saw a Kekeya soldier rushing towards the young man. Arochan just put his sword and shield down when he was kicked on his back by the soldier. Arochan fell onto his face and turned to see the soldier lifting his sword up to make a move onto him.

Mitrajit rushed towards Arochan and blocked the soldier's attack by bringing his shield just in time. He immediately hit back at the soldier with his sword. The soldier was surprised with Mitrajit's intervention. As he fell, blood oozed from the soldier's head, which was split open by Mitrajit's sword. The soldier collapsed down and as he gasped for air, he looked at Mitrajit and said 'Not fair. I was fighting with him.'

Mitrajit got angry hearing those words. He kicked on the chest of the injured soldier and said, 'What is not being fair? You attacked this young man as he was taking a break. You think that was fair?'

Before he could pause, Mitrajit saw another soldier rushing towards him.

Mitrajit, furious at this point, went berserk on the attacking soldier. With both his shield and sword alternating between defending and attacking, he pushed the soldier a few meters back. The soldier tumbled upon the dead bodies and fell. He immediately dropped his sword and brought both hands together asking Mitrajit to spare him.

In the spur of the moment, not realizing that the soldier dropped his sword, Mitrajit went ahead and sliced the soldier's chest. Blood start squirting around, and the soldier's body fell lifeless.

Mitrajit stopped for a second. He realized he didn't follow the rules. He felt gutted for a second that he killed the soldier while he was unarmed.

With a shock on his face, Mitrajit turned around. He saw Arochan watching all this in shock. Mitrajit took big steps to reach Arochan and dropped his weapons.

'I am sorry, dear, for doing that. I didn't realize he dropped his sword. It was too late, I already took position to hit him,' Mitrajit said.

Arochan didn't reply. He was still in shock. He had rarely seen Mitrajit in this kind of a mood. Mitrajit always came across as a calm and wise person and not hot headed like his father. But here he was, kneeling beside him after going wild to kill an unarmed person.

'Look at me, Arochan. I am sorry for what I did, but it was in the spur of the moment. I was angry with this soldier who attacked when you were about to take a break and then this other soldier attacked during that time. It all happened quickly. I hope you understand,' Mitrajit continued to express his intentions to the young man.

Arochan nodded along. 'I can understand, Taatsri. It was just shocking to me to see you like that,' he said.

'Well, this battle is bringing out the beast in all of us. Now let's get going. Are you okay? Do you want to go back to the camp?' Mitrajit asked.

'I am fine. I will continue fighting. Looks like you got injured too.'

'No. A small wound from a stray arrow. I am good. Let's go then,' Mitrajit said as he held the sword and got up.

*****

The fight continued for a few more ghadiyas before it started getting cooler and darker. It was almost sunset time.

Mitrajit never felt so tired before. This was the longest he had ever fought and the pain from his shoulder wasn't helping either. He was curious to see how his old friend was doing. He dropped his sword down and took a break. He looked around for Chitraangad.

A few meters away, he saw Chitraangad fighting valiantly. Mitrajit realized his friend was bleeding from the side of the trunk; it looked like an injury from a stray arrow. Someone should have thought about the stray arrows while writing the rules of the battles, he thought.

Mitrajit was worried for his friend. Chitraangad was someone who would continue fighting without taking a break. He was looking forward to participating in this war and demonstrating his exceptional skills. And right now, he looked to be injured by an arrow and still continued fighting along.

Mitrajit was thinking of getting up when he saw Chitraangad was looking at him from his periphery for a second. He could see Chitraangad smile at him as he continued to fight with the Kekeya soldier. Mitrajit gave a smile back in acknowledgement and signaled him to concentrate on the soldier in front of him.

Taking advantage of that small lapse from Chitraangad, the Kekeya soldier hit Chitraangad with his shield in the face. Chitraangad, surprised by the attack, started to bleed from his nose. The blow shocked him. Before Chitraangad could react, the soldier took his sword and jumped onto him to give another blow.

Chitraangad couldn't hold on to the continuous blows that the soldier was forcing on him. His grip on the shield became weaker and with another blow it fell aside, leaving a gap open in front through which the soldier's sword sliced through to cut Chitraangad's right arm.

Mitrajit watched this in shock as his friend's right arm fell down, cut off from his body along with the sword he was holding.

Chitraangad fell to the ground in pain, clutching onto his right arm with his left hand. The limb below the mid-arm was cut off and blood was oozing out of it quickly.

Mitrajit came rushing towards his friend's side and kicked the soldier aside and hit him with his sword. The soldier collapsed down with that blow to his neck.

Dropping his sword and shield, Mitrajit held Chitraangad in his arms and lifted his friend's body onto his lap. Chitraangad looked at him with pain and tears in his eyes and said, 'Ah there you are. I thought I saw you a few meters away. It was definitely you.'

'Yes, and I am sorry if I distracted you Chitra. This is not what I expected to happen.'

'Well, my friend, I think this is it. I don't think I can fight anymore. I fought as bravely as I could so far... but now...I am feeling weak...I can feel my body getting colder, Mitra.'

Mitrajit looked at the rest of the arm that was left. He immediately removed the waist cloth he was wearing and tightened it around the arm to stop the blood from oozing out, but it didn't look sufficient to stop the flow.

'I am... feeling...thirsty...Mitra. I hope...Arochan is safe...too,' Chitraangad continued to talk.

'Arochan is fine. I was fighting beside him a few ghadiyas earlier. He is brave just like you. He will be fine. Now take this sip of water. I will take you out of here. Let me check for the medic chariot. Be strong,' Mitrajit said as he took his leather pouch out and helped his friend drink water.

Chitraangad had trouble drinking water. 'I am feeling.... cold...Mitra. Looks like I am.... losing it.... I don't know...if I will

see...Subhadra and.... Arochan again...Please take...care of them...
my friend. Everything is.... getting...darker...around...me...'

Mitrajit tried to shake his friend awake. 'No, no. Don't close your
eyes. Look at me. We will go to the camp in the medic chariot right
now and all will be fine,' he said in vain as Chitraangad closed his
eyes and became unconscious.

Mitrajit didn't know what to do. His friend was getting colder.
Was he losing him? Mitrajit checked for the heartbeat, and he could
still feel it faintly coming from his friend's chest.

He looked around for a medic chariot. Far away he saw another
chariot, but not with a green flag with the fire symbol on it. Must be
one of the Maharathi's chariots, he thought. He looked around for
Arochan to see if he was around but couldn't find him. He couldn't
see Aparajit or Viraata, or maybe he was just getting confused with
so many of them fighting around.

He was becoming restless to find a medic chariot. At a distance,
he saw one with the green flag and started shouting hard. He realized
it would be difficult to hear in the middle of all the noise around him.
He got up and started waving while shouting for help.

There were a few other injured soldiers in the vicinity who started
shouting too. That brought attention to one of the charioteers and
he drove the chariot towards them.

As soon as the medic chariot came closer, he took his friend and
placed him at the back of the chariot. He saw four more injured
soldiers at the back. The charioteer looked at Mitrajit's wounded

shoulder and said, 'You look wounded too. Come with me, I need some help to pick a few more wounded soldiers and drop them off.'

Mitrajit was about to climb when he realized that he would be leaving Arochan in the field. He looked at the charioteer and said, 'I can't come, as I have promised to take care of his son.'

'If his son is fighting, he should be taking care of himself. If you are so particular, I can drop you off back at the field once we drop your friend off. There is no time, let me know if you want to come.'

Mitrajit was torn. Should he leave his friend and be here with Arochan or should he go with his unconscious friend and make sure someone attended to him and get back later? Would he have enough time to get back?

He looked around one more time to see if he could find Arochan anywhere close by. He couldn't. *I may not be able to search around for him with everyone fighting. Maybe it is better to be with Chitraangad and try to come back if possible before the sun sets,* he thought.

'Are you coming or not?' the charioteer asked. 'We have to rush as we have to pick up others.'

'Yes, I am coming.' Mitrajit climbed into the chariot and sat beside his unconscious friend. He looked at the four other injured soldiers. Only one of them looked conscious and with minimal cuts on his body while the other three were heavily injured.

The charioteer stopped close to other injured soldiers around the area. Mitrajit helped to pick up more injured soldiers and put them on the chariot.

As they were heading to the camp, Mitrajit silently thanked God for sending the charioteer just in time. Thanks to the wartime rules of not attacking non-combatant chariots and personnel.

The charioteer tried his best to steer away from dead bodies and fallen soldiers. 'More chariots will come to pick you up,' he shouted as they passed injured soldiers. 'We can only take ten of them at a time,' he said, looking at Mitrajit.

Once they reached the end of the battle area, the chariot took a turn to go east towards the Kaurava camp. Mitrajit turned back to look towards the battle zone. Dust was on all the soldiers as they were fighting with each other. He also saw many injured horses and elephants either down on the ground or moving towards the outer zone. He could also see that in some areas, the sky was darker as the arrows covered that area. The dark area would move as it followed the arrows.

'Arochan,' Chitraangad murmured in an unconscious state. Mitrajit looked at his friend and said 'I don't know if you are hearing or not, but don't worry about him. He will be fine. I will go back to check on him as soon as I drop you at the camp.'

A sense of guilt came across for Mitrajit. Was he wrong to leave Arochan and come with Chitraangad in the chariot? Would his friend be fine if he knew this was what he had done? But I couldn't have easily found Arochan in that crowd and with the time being almost sunset, the battles may end soon, he thought.

*****

MANU NELLUTLA

Purna woke up just after sunrise that morning. Acharya ji announced the previous day that gurukul would be closed for a few days as the kids were not able to concentrate on the studies. Everyone was eager to hear about their fathers' and brothers' status from the battles. As per the messenger's information the war must have started a few minutes back.

Immediately, Purna folded her hands and prayed. 'Oh Lord Shiva, I have never asked anything substantive to you in many years. All I ask is to keep my father safe. Please bring him home safely. Not just him but everyone else too, including brother Arochan.'

She got up from the bed to freshen up. As she went across the verandah of the home towards the washroom, she saw that her mother was lighting lamps at the pooja altar.

'Go take a bath and come. Let us pray before we start our day today,' Dhruti told Purna.

Purna took no time in getting ready and came to sit near her mother. Both sat quietly for some time praying.

After the pooja, to change the focus of their minds, Dhruti said, 'Let's play Astapada[81]. It has been a while since we played.'

'Yes, good idea.'

While playing, Purna asked, 'Amma, what if something happens to pitashri? What are we going to do?'

Dhruti was surprised to hear that question. 'Why would you ask that? What made you think that way?'

---

[81] Precursor to Chess

'Well, while I was playing yesterday, Bhumi was mentioning that her mother said they might go back to their maternal place if anything happens to their father. Even Suvarna was saying the same thing. I said that we have not planned anything like that as I know pitashri will come back.'

'Well, that is a good attitude you have, Purna. Always think and wish for a positive outcome. Now that you ask me, I think we should still discuss what we should be doing if at all the outcomes of the war are not how we would have expected.'

'I know that pitashri is going to come back safely. I have been praying daily too. I told my friends too that we are not going to plan anything different as I have full faith that pitashri will be back safely. And moreover, today is just the first day and I don't want us to talk about the outcome yet. We will get more information from the messengers soon.'

Dhruti looked at Purna with pity. She agreed with her point that all they could do was hope for Mitrajit to return. But it wasn't as easy as their hope. They had to be prepared for the worst-case scenario.

'I understand your frustration, dear. I am with you on this. At the same time, let us think about what your father would do. He would have plans for various scenarios. He even made sure our barn was properly filled with grain before he left so that in case of necessity, we could survive. The whole village is still under patrol as you never know when Ekapaadas may attack. So, we should also plan ahead and see if we are prepared enough for any scenario.'

'You always use pitashri's examples to cut me off.'

'Ha-ha. Not at all. I use pitashri's actions as example because we both know he makes wise choices, and we respect him for that.'

'Okay,' Purna continued, 'you win. So, do you have any ideas already?'

'Well, me and Subhadra were talking, and we both felt that maybe we should head back to Keertipuram, my father's place. Though we have not been there for many years, at least we can feel that we can call that place one of ours. I don't know though if they were called upon to participate in the war as they were close to the Asmakas.'

'Oh. I heard from acharya ji that the Asmakas may be participating on the Pandava side. I would hate to think Keertipuram people will be on their side and fighting against us.'

'Well, I have no idea, but I don't think it affects our relationship with whoever is fighting on either side. Even the cousins themselves are fighting each other.'

'True,' Purna slowly said. 'But I still hope that pitashri comes back safely.'

'Of course, dear. Now move your horse to this black square if you don't want me to pin your King,' Dhruti said to bring Purna's attention back to the game.

*****

'We are here,' the charioteer announced. 'Please help me in getting these soldiers to the tents.'

Mitrajit jumped down from the chariot and saw there were other non-combatant personnel waiting for them to take the injured soldiers to the tents. One of them came to assist him in taking Chitraangad inside. After seeing Chitraangad, he said to Mitrajit, 'Looks like he has lost lots of blood. Let's take him inside quickly. Did you get the rest of the cut off limb? We could salvage it if it's still fresh.'

Mitrajit looked at the person and said, 'No,' with guilt in his eyes. He never thought to take the cut off limb.

Looking at Mitrajit's face, the person replied, 'Don't worry. I was just asking as per the routine. The medics sometimes ask for the cut off part.' They both picked Chitraangad in a cart and started moving towards the tent.

The charioteer came running towards Mitrajit. 'Thanks for your help. Let me know if you want to get back to the warfront. I will leave in a few minutes. Though I can see that it is almost time the conches will be blown to signal the end of the day's war. Still, up to you. I will wait for few more minutes before I head back. You can meet me here if you want to go.'

Mitrajit nodded and replied, 'Thank you for your timely help. I will come out and check soon.'

Once inside the tent, Mitrajit saw scores of injured soldiers being treated. Some of them had amputated arms and limbs while others were in an unconscious state. Some of the soldiers' bodies were cleaned by men to remove blood-soaked dust from the bodies. Some others were screaming in pain. It looked like a scene from naraka[82].

Mitrajit put Chitraangad on an empty mat while a vaidya got a pan with water to clean the body and the arm stump. He tied Chitraangad's arm stump with a fresh cloth just above the cut part to minimize the bleeding. The vaidya looked at Mitrajit and said, 'Please stay outside and I will let you know in a ghadiya about the prognosis.'

Outside the tent, Mitrajit saw a big tank with water. It was like the one they had at the village for the cows and goats to come and drink water. He went there to wash the dust and blood that was on him. He felt a sharp pain as he washed his arms. The cuts from the sword fighting, though not deep, were causing the pain as the dust came off from them. All this time, the dust was covering the wounds. As he washed his shoulder area, he noticed swelling at the area where the arrow hit him. He tried to move his shoulder and he was able to, though not easily. Nothing much to worry about, he thought.

He looked around. The scene around the medical tents was chaotic, with medic chariots coming in with injured soldiers. He looked for the charioteer who dropped them off but couldn't see him anywhere close. There was one person who was giving directions and orders to other personnel. Must be a General, Mitrajit thought.

---

[82] Hell

Mitrajit went to that General and said, 'Excuse me, sir. I am one of the Ustrakarnikas fighting alongside the Kalingas. I just came back from the battle to help my injured friend to be brought to the camp. He is in the tent checked upon by the medics. I would like to know if I can rejoin the battle and go in one of the chariots heading way back in.'

The General looked at Mitrajit. 'You want to go back?' he said with a surprised look on his face. 'I don't think that is possible now. It would be tough to drop you off where you want to be. The troops must have moved ahead from the place where you were earlier at. We got reports that the Pandava armies couldn't cross onto our side, thanks to the fierce battle from Bhishma and others. Even if you go, by the time you reach our army and try to go to the forefront, it will be sunset. You look injured too. Better get them looked at today so you can get back fresh tomorrow.'

Mitrajit was a bit disappointed. He was worried that he wasn't around Arochan. The General got back to giving orders to the charioteers. Everyone around looked busy.

Mitrajit was feeling desperate. He sat down in front of the tent and kept his gaze towards the battle ground. Anytime now the conches would be blown, and he wanted to make sure Arochan was back safely. As he was waiting, tiredness crept upon him, and he fell asleep.

He was awakened suddenly by the sounds of the conches announcing the end of the first day's battles. Mitrajit was anxious to know what happened and to see if Arochan was safe. But before that, he wanted to check upon the vaidya to get an update on his friend.

'The bleeding stopped, and the wound is looking good. May heal well, though it will take some days until the bandages can come off totally. He lost a lot of blood that made him to go into a state of shock, hence the unconsciousness. My men will help you to take him to your camp. I will pass by tomorrow to change his bandages. If he gains consciousness, though I don't know how soon that will be, give him lots of liquids so that he can recover,' the vaidya informed.

Mitrajit thanked the medic and took his friend to their tent with the help of others. He put a pillow under Chitraangad's head and whispered to him, 'Feel good my friend. I want to see us go back to our village to our families and grow old together. Don't worry about Arochan. I know he will be safe there. He is a brave warrior just like his father.'

Mitrajit came out of the tent and waited for the troops to come back. Many soldiers from the Kalinga and Narayani sena started arriving. He saw Aparajit coming towards the tents with a few other Ustrakarnikas. Behind him was Viraata and following him was Arochan, drenched in blood but walking normally.

Mitrajit was relieved to see Arochan safe. At the same time, he was worried as to how the young man would react to his father's condition.

Arochan saw Mitrajit at the tent and came running towards him. 'Thank God you are here. We were looking for you and pitashri all over. Where is he? I am worried for him.'

'Yes, it's a relief to see you here. Where is Chitraangad? I hope he is safe too,' Aparajit said as he followed behind Arochan. Everyone else started getting around Mitrajit.

Mitrajit looked at them with a grim face and replied, 'He is safe but he got injured and he is now taking rest in the tent', he said as he pointed towards their tent.

'What happened to him?' Arochan asked but didn't wait for the answer as he ran into the tent.

'How seriously injured is he?' Aparajit asked.

'He is unconscious right now as he lost a lot of blood. He lost his right arm in the battle,' Mitrajit said with a heavy voice.

Aparajit put a hand on Mitrajit's shoulder. 'Oh God. Hope he recovers soon. Today we have lost so many already.'

Mitrajit looked towards Aparajit. 'How many?'

'At least two hundred men, I think, as many have been still unaccounted for. I will take a roll order soon and we will get an idea.'

Mitrajit dropped his head down and buried it in both hands. 'That's a lot for just one day,' he said, shocked at the number. They had never lost so many men on one day, even when there were long drawn battles with the Ekapaadas.

'Let me go in and check on Chitraangad,' Aparajit said. Mitrajit followed him.

Inside the tent, Arochan was devastated to see his father lying unconscious on the mat with bandages around his arm stump. He looked at Mitrajit and spoke. 'I didn't expect to see him like this. What happened? What will happen to us now? How can we tell mother about this? How will she take this news? She will be devastated.' Arochan couldn't control his tears and cried as he hugged Mitrajit.

Mitrajit took a deep breath and said, 'I am sorry about this, son. He was fighting bravely until he got distracted for a moment and the opposing Kekeya soldier took an opportunity to swing and cut his arm. I was close by and was able to bring him here. The vaidya said that he lost lots of blood and hence is in an unconscious state. They will check on him tomorrow and they were positive that he'll regain consciousness anytime. Let us all pray and hope that he will recover quickly,' Mitrajit replied while hoping that the thathaastu devatas would hear him out.

Aparajit came towards them and said, 'This is sad, but at least we should be thankful that he is alive and safe. Be with him and I will come after dinner to check. I will have to go now to get updates and make arrangements for the cremation of our fellow men we have lost today.'

Mitrajit looked at Aparajit and said, 'I can come to help, if you want.'

'No. You stay here. You need rest too. I will connect with you later. Take care of them.'

Mitrajit nodded and looked towards his friend Arochan. 'Arochan, go and get freshened up. We can take turns to sit here. Don't worry, he will be fine. You know what a brave man he is.'

Arochan looked at Mitrajit and said, 'Thanks for saving my life today in the middle out there.'

'Ah. That was my duty to protect you dear. Me and your father promised each other to protect you as much as possible from our end. Anyways, all is well now. At least we are all safe.'

*****

That evening, Mitrajit struggled to meditate. It took some time for him to concentrate as the shoulder injury from the arrow started to bother him. As he slowly went into a state of deep meditation, the words he said to Arochan came back to his mind. At least we are all safe. Mitrajit felt guilty for saying those words. He was being selfish at that moment. Around two hundred of his fellow Ustrakarnikas died and he was talking about being safe. He felt restless. Should he be happy for surviving the day, for his friend to still be alive and Arochan to be still alive or should he be sad that they lost so many of his people just on the first day of the war? He himself had killed so many soldiers. What about their families? Mitrajit tried hard to concentrate and meditate.

After meditating sometime, Mitrajit went to check up with Aparajit. With Chitraangad injured and unconscious, Aparajit may be missing the usual support he would get, Mitrajit thought.

Mitrajit found Aparajit talking to various generals outside the tents.

Aparajit turned around towards Mitrajit and said, 'There you are. Hope the kid and Chitraangad are doing well. I was following up with these generals in charge of the chariots. They are going to take all the dead bodies to the outskirts of the zone for cremation. I have tasked Viraata and Maarthanda to identify our men among the piles of dead bodies. We should keep a list so that we can also communicate and prepare for proper rituals once back home.'

No matter what the situation, Aparajit always looked in control. That's what a good leader is, Mitrajit thought.

Mitrajit nodded and said, 'Sure. Let me know how I can be of help. I know you may be missing Chitraangad to help you with all these things.'

Aparajit gave a smile and replied, 'I am glad you asked, Mitra. I didn't want to burden you at this time as it may be shocking for you seeing Chitraangad in that state. The only positive news from today is that Chitraangad is still alive. We have lost so many of our men today. I don't want the morale of our people go down. I want your support tomorrow to rally our troops. The Kalingas think that today was a win for the Kaurava camp. Though the continuous assault from the Pandavas, especially from Bheema and the arrows from Arjuna, made it difficult for all of us, we should be thankful to Bhishma who arrived to support us just in time and deterred the Pandava brothers' push towards us. He alone neutralized many threats from the opposing army thus saving many of us today. Still, I didn't expect for us to lose so many men. This war is definitely at a totally different level than what I expected it would be.'

'This is a huge loss for us. We have never lost so many men. I too didn't expect this war to be so fierce and engaging. It has been a full day of continuous fighting. I will be there in the morning to rally the troops. Do you need help with cremation, or any other things?'

'I think we are fine for now. We all need to rest up and feel fresh tomorrow. Your face looks pale. Make sure you rest well. Let me finish the rituals and then go meet the Kalinga commanders. They may have more updates for both today's events and tomorrow's strategies. I will meet you right after to update you.'

At dinner, everyone was quiet. Viraata came and sat beside Mitrajit. 'It was a tough fight today. This is what I was worried about, Mitra. I hope you can relate to this now,' he said, trying to justify his outburst the day before.

'I agree with you, Viraata. But we are here now, and we will continue fighting. The rest of us will fight hard. Aparajit said that today's fight was a good one for our side. Hopefully the good tide continues tomorrow too. The sooner we can end this war, the earlier we can get out of this,' Mitrajit replied.

'And then what message do you think we should send to Devasthana about the men we lost today? Losing around two hundred men in one day may be normal for the larger armies like the Kalingas, but for us it's devastating,' Virata said.

Mitrajit looked at him and said, 'I agree with you, Viraata, that it is not going to be easy with messaging back home. But what surprises me is that you are back to questioning our purpose here; it will not help those who are already sulking with the news. You are more than welcome to leave even now, Viraata, but don't discourage others.'

Viraata kept quiet, understanding that Mitrajit was serious. 'Sorry again,' he said.

Mitrajit didn't reply. He didn't want to. He was already tired from the battle. Seeing his friend unconscious, hearing the news of losing their men and now the continuous discussion about participation in this war. That tide had passed many days ago. All he wanted was some peace and rest.

After dinner, Aparajit came to check on Chitraangad.

'He is still unconscious. We've been putting on these medications given to us by the vaidya. One of them came earlier to check and say that his pulse has improved, and he has given these patches to put on Chitra's skin so·that he can receive necessary nutrition and energy through skin absorption,' Mitrajit updated Aparajit on his friend's condition.

'Good to know. The medical system has always been evolving. Never heard of medicine that can be absorbed by the skin directly before. Glad they can help. Can you come out to discuss a few things?'

Mitrajit and Aparajit went outside the tent. 'The Kalingas are sending messengers back home to provide updates. I was thinking that we would not send any updates from our end, especially about what happened today. I don't want our people to be shocked about first day's loss. They will be worried about it the next few days. The Kalingas said that we are in good position in the war and may finish off the Pandava armies by tomorrow or by third day. So, I feel that we should send the message that all is well and that we feel that we can turn the tide soon. What do you think?' Aparajit asked.

Mitrajit was surprised by the suggestion of his leader. But then he appreciated why Aparajit might have wanted to send this message. He would not have wanted to send panic among the villagers. 'Makes sense. We will see how it looks over the next few days and then update accordingly,' he replied.

'Good. I will inform them. Meanwhile I got information that we will be taking the Garuda Vyuha[83] in tomorrow's battle. We will again be on the right wing of this eagle shaped formation. Please inform the rest of our people. How is everyone doing so far?' Aparajit inquired.

'Everyone was quiet except for Viraata, who has been questioning our participation again. He got riled up after today's losses. I told him that he is more than welcome to leave if he wants to but not continue with that thought and disrupt everyone.'

'Good call. If he bothers you anymore then let me know, I may want to dismiss him altogether from the camp. We don't want anyone else to demoralize us again,' Aparajit replied. 'Now go ahead and get a good night's sleep. I will join you all again in the morning.'

'You too. It has been long day for you.'

'Thanks, Mitra,' Aparajit said as he gave a hug to Mitrajit. 'I was tensed for few minutes when I couldn't find you and Chitraangad at

---

[83] Strategy/ Formation in Eagle shape

the battle zone. I was worried that I must have lost you both. I am now glad to see you both alive even though Chitra got injured.'

Mitrajit was surprised with the sudden emotional hug from Aparajit. The old man is also going through a lot of stress, he realized. 'I am glad too that we could survive today's onslaught but also sad to lose our men.'

Aparajit eased on the hug and said, 'It is the price we have to pay for the bigger cause, Mitra. Now let us go and take rest.'

Mitrajit had a hard time sleeping that night. He couldn't digest the fact that he was the reason Chitraangad got distracted for a second that led to him being attacked. He tossed from side to side on his bed. Unable to sleep, he got up to check on Arochan and Chitraangad. Arochan was lying down beside his father's bed. He was there beside him the whole evening. Thank God, I was able to intervene to protect Arochan today, Mitrajit thought.

Mitrajit went back to try to sleep. His thoughts took him to Purna and Dhruti. They might be looking forward to any message from the messengers. His thoughts slowly meandered towards the battlefield. What a day it had been! 'Oh Lord Shiva, please bless the souls of the men whom I had to kill as part of this war. I was doing what was my dharma and keeping myself alive,' he prayed as he slowly went deep into sleep.

8.Vajraghaata[84] Parva

Mitrajit woke up early in the morning with pain in his right shoulder. He removed the top cloth on his body to see that the spot where the arrow hit was swollen with pus. *Perhaps the wound got infected*, he thought. 'Should have gotten it checked yesterday,' he murmured under his breath while getting angry with himself for not taking care of it. He tried to move his shoulder but the swelling didn't allow him to.

He got up to see everyone else getting ready. He realized he must have overslept. He went over to check Chitraangad and Arochan. Arochan was still sleeping beside his father. Mitrajit tapped on Arochan's shoulder to wake him up.

---

[84] Shock/Shocking outcomes

Arochan woke up and saw Mitrajit beside him. 'Oh sorry. I didn't notice it was morning already.'

Mitrajit saw Arochan's face and said, 'I didn't realize either. You look very tired and pale. Looks like you didn't sleep well.'

Arochan looked at Mitrajit and felt the warmth in his words. He always looked up to Mitrajit as his hero. For him, Mitrajit was more than just his father's friend. He was like the uncle he never had. Mitrajit, Purna and Dhruti were so much part of their family too.

'Now go ahead and freshen up. I will talk to Aparajit about you staying in today to be with your father,' Mitrajit continued.

'No, that is fine. I can go and participate in the battle. It will be odd for me to stay here with my father when others are fighting.'

'We will look into it. I can't send you to fight when you are in this state,' Mitrajit replied.

Arochan looked at him for a second. Mitrajit was right. He was not in a state to go and fight a war with little to no rest overnight. He nodded in agreement with Mitrajit. 'I am sorry, Taatsri. I tried my best but couldn't sleep.'

'It is fine, my dear. Totally understandable. Now go and freshen up. I will stay here with your father.'

As Arochan went out of the tent, Mitrajit sat down beside his friend. Chitraangad's face looked better this morning. *The medicines must be working their magic,* he thought.

Mitrajit got up and tried to stretch his body. He still had a tough time moving his shoulder.

Aparajit entered the tent and saw Mitrajit struggling. 'Looks like you didn't get it checked yesterday,' he said.

'No. But it should be okay by the time we are summoned to line up. I just need to warm up a bit.'

'Let me look at it,' Aparajit said and came closer to inspect the shoulder area. 'Lord Shiva, it is infected.' He touched Mitrajit's forehead. 'And your body is warm too.'

'It is nothing. I should be fine, but I wanted to ask if Arochan can stay with Chitra. He hasn't slept properly the whole night and I am bothered to send him to the battle in that condition.'

'Of course, that makes sense. I also want you to stay along with him. Get that shoulder checked by a vaidya and get treated. If you are feeling better by tomorrow you can participate, but of course that depends if the war is still on as we may finish it off by today,' Aparajit ended that sentence with a smile.

'I should be fine; I can be there to support you and the troops.'

'Nonsense. I don't want to hear anything else. I can manage the troops along with others. Your shoulder needs to heal. This is my decision. Both you and Arochan will stay here at the tent and help everyone else. I also want you to check with the vaidya as soon as possible.'

Mitrajit looked down. He couldn't argue. Aparajit was right. He should have gotten the shoulder checked out yesterday. At least he could have been in good enough shape today to fight.

'It is okay, Mitra. Now take care of Chitraangad and I will see you all in the evening.'

After informing Arochan about Aparajit's decision, Mitrajit came out to talk to the troops. Even if he was not participating, he could at least motivate them and be there to help Aparajit as needed.

Aparajit was gathering everyone to discuss the strategies for the day when he saw Mitrajit. 'There you are. Always standing by with your men. Glad you are not in your military attire. I was about to talk to the troops. Be here with me and send us on our way to the battlefront,' he said with a smile.

'Hail Lord Shiva. My fellow Ustrakarnikas, yesterday was a glimpse of what a great war we are participating in. Along with our friends Kalingas and others in the Kaurava camp, we were able to thwart the Pandava allies, especially the Kekeyas. We also suffered losses. But the sacrifices that our men made will not go in vain. I am confident after yesterday's battles that Ustrakarnikas are mighty and strong enough to fight with anyone in this world.' Aparajit was rallying up his troops with these encouraging words.

'Today we will be taking Garuda Vyuha,' Aparajit continued. 'This time behind the elephant unit of the Kalingas. This will also be advantageous to us as the enemies themselves and their morale will be trampled by the elephants by the time they reach us. Now let us go and show what Ustrakarnikas are made of. Hail Lord Shiva.'

Everyone around him shouted, 'Hail Lord Shiva. Victory to us. Hail Lord Shiva.'

Aparajit went towards Mitrajit and said, 'You must not have noticed but Viraata has left the camp alone. It seems he decided he doesn't want to fight anymore. I didn't get a chance to see him as he had already left by the time. I can see that it had little effect on our men; most of them are eager to get back and fight after yesterday's victory.'

'Oh, that's unfortunate. I hope he will realize his mistake. I don't know how he will face us once we are back home. We will see,' Mitrajit replied.

'Yes. Now let me go and God willing I will see you in the evening sound and safe,' Aparajit said.

'Hail Lord Shiva. He will protect you all.'

After the troops left to assemble in lines, Mitrajit went to the medic tents. On the way there, he saw the Narayani sena getting ready for their positions. He saw Aayusha waving at him and went to meet him.

'Nice to see you again, Mitrajit,' Aayusha said. 'Aren't you participating in the battles today?'

'I hurt my shoulder from a stray arrow and it got infected. I was heading to the medic tent to get it looked at.'

'Oh, okay. Hope it heals soon. By the way, now that you are here, let me introduce you to my general.'

Aayusha turned around to speak to a person who by his war attire looked to be a high-ranking soldier.

'He is my general and mentor, Satyavan. I owe everything to him. He is my guide and philosopher too. Sir, he is Mitrajit. One of the Ustrakarnikas. He is with Aparajit.'

Satyavan smiled while patting on Aayusha's shoulder and said, 'Ah. Always ready to flatter me. Nice to meet you, Mitrajit. I am glad we were able to fight together in this war. I have high regard for the swordsmanship of your tribe.'

'Thank you for your kind words,' Mitrajit replied. 'I am glad to meet you too. You have got a bright and well-mannered young man working with you,' he said, pointing towards Aayusha.

'Oh, yeah. He is one of our best,' Satyavan replied. 'Now that I am in a hurry to leave for the battle, let us meet, hopefully, in the evening for dinner. I would like to hear more about the Ustrakarnikas.'

'Sure, General. Nice seeing you again, Aayusha. I wish you all the very best and hope that you all return safely.' Mitrajit wished them well and continued heading towards the medic tent.

At the medic tent, one of the vaidya took a heated knife tip and punctured the swelling on Mitrajit's shoulder. He then put a patch of herbs and informed him to come back again in the afternoon for a change of patch. He also gave Mitrajit a drink to reduce the fever from infection. Ustrakarnikas only had a vaidya when he was younger, but since then it was the acharya who with some knowledge about medicinal herbs would help them out with any health issues. Seeing a well sophisticated medical unit made Mitrajit think about the benefits of being part of a big kingdom.

Just as Mitrajit came out of the tent, he heard the conches being blown. Slowly the dust started rising on the western side, which was changing into an orangish gold color while reflecting the rays of the rising sun from the east.

'Lord Shiva, protect my fellow brothers out there,' Mitrajit prayed silently.

He went towards their camp and saw Arochan sitting outside, looking towards the battle ground. 'Let us go to the hillock we went to the other day, and we may get a better view of the battle zone. We can come in between to check on Chitra,' Mitrajit said to the young man.

'That is a good idea. I never got to see the scale of the war yesterday as we were on the ground fighting. All I could see was a few meters around me.'

'Of course. Let us go then. We can tell the guard to let us know if Chitra wakes up.'

At the hillock, they saw some other people sitting and watching the battlefield. They were taking notes. Probably observers or historians noting down the live events, Mitrajit assumed.

From the top, Mitrajit couldn't believe what he was seeing. From South to North across the western side of the camp, the ground was filled with troops, elephants, horses, chariots, and flags all blurred behind a layer of rising dust. There were continuous clanking sounds from the swords. In between the dust clouds, he could see lightning. Perhaps the advanced weapons everyone was dreading about being used by the maharathis, he thought.

Arochan watched all this for a while in shock. The grand canvas laid in front of the young man painted a picture he could have never dreamt of. He was still young when the Ekapaadas last attacked Devasthana. All he knew about wars was through reading in the books. But here he was, soaking it all in as it happened in front of him.

By afternoon, both Mitrajit and Arochan took turns to check on Chitraangad. There was not much change in him. Mitrajit also got a chance to change the bandage patch on his shoulder. The vaidya helped move the shoulder and it seemed to be moving smoothly compared to the morning. He encouraged Mitrajit to keep moving his shoulder so that it would feel better by evening.

As he was leaving the medic tent, Mitrajit could see more injured soldiers being brought to the tents. He could see some of the soldiers going back to the battleground on the empty medic chariots once looked after by the medics. *Wish I could go too*, Mitrajit thought as he was still concerned about his men and Aparajit.

*****

Dhruti and Subhadra went to Kumudini's house after lunch. Everyone in Devasthana was eagerly waiting for any news from the warfront.

'I don't think we will have any news today. Perhaps tomorrow,' Kumudini said to them.

An expression of disappointment could be seen on their faces upon hearing that update.

'I am sorry that this is not what you wanted to hear. I will check with Mareechi if he has any other information.'

'No issues. It is not in our hands. We are dependent on the Kalingas to pass on the information. Anyways, we should try and get things going as we must finish harvesting crops soon,' Dhruti replied.

'True. I also don't want the villagers to get back into a worrisome mood. They were all engaged with the activities we have been organizing in the past few days.' Kumudini was keen to keep the Ustrakarnikas engaged with activities.

'Yes. Let's get things organized for tomorrow's sahapankti bhojanam[85]. That will get their spirits high. What are you planning to cook?' Subhadra asked.

'Nothing planned yet, but maybe a dessert.'

'No surprise that Devasthana's dessert specialist would prepare a dessert for all of us. I am eager to see what you may bring.' Dhruti always appreciated the desserts that Kumudini would prepare.

Everyone burst into laughter. It was a good way to keep their thoughts away from the stress of the war and now with no news yet, they were worried but trying their best to hide their feelings.

*****

After lunch, Mitrajit went and sat on the hillock again. He could see the Kalinga army's elephant unit moving around, the howdahs on top of them visible due to their bright colors. After a few

---

[85] Community lunch/Get together

moments, he saw those howdahs falling. He tried to focus in that area to see what was happening. One after the other, the elephants in the unit went down. There was a lot of dust from that area. He could see some of the elephants running towards the north side without a howdah on their tops. *Their mahouts[86] must have been killed, along with the warriors sitting on the top of the howdahs,* Mitrajit thought.

The other observers were murmuring something. Mitrajit looked towards them and heard them mention Bheema more than twice. Bheema, the second of the Pandava brothers, was very famous for his superhuman strength. 'He must be creating havoc among the elephant unit,' they mentioned.

Mitrajit observed more dust and chaos on the northern end of the ground. That was where the Kalinga and the Narayani sena were fighting along with the Ustrakarnikas. 'Lord Shiva, please keep protecting them,' he prayed silently.

After some time, he came down to check on Chitraangad. Arochan was sleeping beside him, taking much needed rest. Mitrajit sat beside them and couldn't resist as he slowly fell into sleep.

Mitrajit was jolted out of sleep by sounds outside the tent. Arochan looked at him and said, 'Looks like the medications started affecting you. By the time I woke up, you were taking a nap and I didn't want to disturb you. Glad you could get some rest too.'

Mitrajit smiled. 'What are those sounds outside?' he inquired.

'No idea. I was just changing the sheets under pitashri's bed.'

---

[86] Keeper or driver of an elephant.

'Let me go and check,' Mitrajit said as he got up and stretched. Mitrajit came out of the tent and was surprised to see General Pattabhadra sitting outside the tents. He had an expression of shock on his face and was looking straight towards the warzone. Mitrajit went towards him and asked, 'My friend, what happened? What are you doing here? Are you okay?'

Pattabhadra turned towards Mitrajit. He could see tears rolling down the general's eyes. Mitrajit braced himself for bad news.

Pattabhadra saw Mitrajit beside him and took a deep breath. 'Oh, Mitra. What has the Lord brought upon us? We are done here. Our great King Srutayush and Prince Sakradeva have been slain today in the battle. We may not even be able to recover Prince Sakradeva's body as the news is that it was smashed into pieces by Bheema's mace. We lost most of our commanders and soldiers. I think most of your men are also killed. Bheema was very aggressive in the field today. He and his soldiers killed everyone they came across. He didn't even leave the elephants. He killed so many of them, too. My friends, the other generals Ketumat, Satya and Satyadeva are also killed. Only a few of us left now from the great Kalinga army. We are lost. Our kingdom is lost.'

Mitrajit couldn't believe it. It was just the second day of the war. His thoughts immediately took him to the words that Pattabhadra said about Ustrakarnikas having been lost. *What would have happened to them? How bad is it? What about Aparajit, Maarthanda and others?*

'Sorry to hear, Pattabhadra. I am lost for words. Do you know anything else about my people? What about Aparajit?'

'It's all done, Mitra. We all have lost everyone we know today. I have not seen him, but I know the unit with Aparajit was destroyed. I hope he is safe though. Where is Chitraangad? I heard about him last night. Hope he is recovering.'

Mitrajit nodded slightly in answer to Pattabhadra's question. He was not in a state to talk any further. *Is the situation really that bad?*

Mitrajit's thoughts kept on wandering to Aparajit as he went towards their tent He was not just the head of the tribe and the villages; he was more like a father figure to him and Chitraangad. Chitraangad, who was now lying unconscious without any idea how devastating the second day had been for them.

Arochan came out to see Mitrajit in a tensed expression. He immediately guessed that something had gone wrong.

Mitrajit looked at Arochan and noticed the doubt on the young man's face. He signaled him to come towards him. Mitrajit repeated what he had heard from General Pattabhadra.

'That is absolutely shocking. How bad it can be? I hope they are safe. I hope Sudeepa is fine', Arochan was worried about his dearest friend. 'Did you hear anything about Aparajit?' he inquired, knowing that Mitrajit would be worried for the chieftain. His father would be too if he was conscious.

'I don't know anything yet. We will have to wait to see. Pattabhadra says it was so bad that only a few of them could come back alive and that most of our men lost their lives in the attack from Bheema. I don't want to ask him or others anything more. They all must be in shock themselves. All we can do is wait for Aparajit and others to come back safely. It's almost time for sunset. Oh, Lord Shiva….' he said as he put his hands together as if he was begging the Lord to spare the lives of his fellow men.

Slowly the sounds from the conches to declare the end of the day's battles started reaching them. Mitrajit and Arochan looked towards the west in anticipation.

The troops started trickling in back to the camp. Most of them were from the Narayani sena. They could see a few dozen Kalingas in between who went straight to talk to Pattabhadra. Still no sign of Ustrakarnikas.

'Maarthanda,' Arochan said as he saw one of their people coming towards the tents. Mitrajit could see the silhouette and couldn't recognize him. Apart from his aging vision, the tears and tense mood didn't help with his eyesight.

Slowly, Maarthanda walked towards Mitrajit and Arochan. He looked exhausted, dust lumps mixed with blood on his body that dried up throughout the day.

Looking at Mitrajit and Arochan, Maarthanda ran and kneeled beside them. The day's fight has taken its toll on his body too.

'It's all over, Mitra. We have lost an entire generation of men. Aparajit is seriously hurt and was taken on a medic chariot. No one is left. Everyone has been killed by Bheema and his troops. Some of them who could survive his onslaught got trampled upon by the wild elephants running astray. I escaped, luckily. I doubt any of the Kalingas survived too. Only the Narayani sena could give a fight to that angry warrior. I am sorry to give this news. I have no idea what we can do now. I am tired.'

Mitrajit took a deep breath. He kneeled beside Maarthanda. Arochan had no idea how to respond. He stood there in shock, looking at the few soldiers that had returned from the battle zone today to the Kalinga's camp and their tents.

'Prayers to Lord Shiva. We all did what we could. Only He knows what is happening or going to happen. Sorry to hear all this. General Pattabhadra of the Kalinga army updated me a few minutes back. It is shocking. You take rest while I go check on Aparajit's condition. I hope we will have some more of our men return,' Mitra said with some hope.

'I doubt it, Mitra. But yes, you better go and check on Aparajit. I hope he is safe.' Maarthanda looked at Arochan and asked, 'How is Chitra doing now? I hope he is recovering.'

Arochan nodded in silence. He was still shocked at the news and the events unfolding before him. He was not able to digest the fact that none of their men returned except for Maarthanda and an injured Aparajit. He was devastated with the thought that he would never see his friends including Sudeepa, his best friend since childhood. Arochan slowly went back towards Chitraangad's tent.

Mitrajit ran towards the medic camp. A sense of deep pain was rising in his mind as he made his way towards the tents. Maybe Viraata was right? Maybe this was a wrong decision. Maybe they should have protested Kalinga's request to participate in this war. Maybe they should have dealt with the Ekapaadas themselves. What were the Ustrakarnikas as a tribe without any of their people? So many thoughts were rushing into his mind and he tried his best to fight them away. His main concern for now had to be Aparajit's condition.

He could see scores of injured soldiers being brought towards the medic camp in the chariots. It would be difficult to find Aparajit immediately. He looked around to see who he should be inquiring about.

Suddenly, he heard his name being called by a familiar voice from one of the tents. He looked in that direction and saw Aayusha. He looked injured, his pierced armor exposing the cuts on his chest.

Mitrajit went towards the injured young man. 'Sorry to see you in this state, Aayusha. You should get attended to by a medic.'

'I am fine, Mitrajit. Much better compared to everyone else. Today was a tough day. If you are looking for Aparajit, he was taken into that tent,' he said pointing towards where he was taken. 'He looked in pretty bad shape.'

"Thanks, Aayusha. I will go and check. Take care of yourself.'

Mitrajit went towards the tent that Aayusha pointed at and saw many injured soldiers on the beds. If this was the number of injured, he was worried at the thought of how many might have been killed.

He found Aparajit being attended by a medic. Aparajit had bandages across his throat and many areas of his chest. Aparajit looked conscious but was having troubles breathing. Looking at Mitrajit, he waved his hand slowly to tell Mitrajit to sit beside him and held his hand.

'Nice to...see you... Mitra...,' Aparajit was gasping for air as he talked with bandages trying to stop the bleeding around his throat.

The medic intervened. 'You should not be talking now. You need rest.'

'I need to...talk...' he said as he signed Mitrajit to come closer him. 'I think we.... are done my son...We lost... this battle. We.... have lost most.... of our men. There could be only.... a couple of us left from our.... tribe and I don't know to how long I can survive.... with these injuries. I feel that.... my time has come. Please take the lead of our.... people. I don't have my own...... kin to give that responsibility.... but then, you are like my own. Take Arochan and .... anyone else left back...... to the village. Hope Chitraangad.... recovers soon too. We need at least ...... some of the men to...... support our tribe. Tell... Kumudini that I.... will meet her.... in heaven. Tell her...... that her husband...... fought bravely.... and she.... can be.... proud of him.'

Those were his last words and Mitrajit could feel the warmth being lost from Aparajit's hands. Aparajit's eyes were open, but there was no life in them. The medics moved Mitrajit aside and covered Aparajit's face with a cloth once they confirmed there was no heartbeat left in him.

Everything around him started to fade a bit. His mentor, leader, fatherly figure Aparajit was no more. His best friend, brother-like Chitraangad was injured and lying unconscious. Now it was only him, Chitraangad, along with Arochan and Maarthanda and hopefully a few more of the Ustrakarnikas left, out of the thousands who came here. It was just the second day of the war. How could they survive back home with no men to support their families? Mitrajit felt his heart beating faster and felt his head pounding. He passed out and collapsed on the ground.

*****

When he opened his eyes, he saw a medic standing beside him. 'You must have fainted. Here, drink some water from the cup,' the medic offered.

Mitrajit took a sip and looked for Aparajit. He was being taken away outside the tent to be placed at the outskirts of the camp where all dead soldiers would be cremated with proper rituals later in the evening.

'Looks like you need to change your bandage too. It is better to get it done before it starts infecting,' the medic said.

Mitrajit nodded in agreement. The medic changed the healing patch on the shoulder. 'It's looking better. It should heal in the next two to three days,' he said.

'Thank you,' Mitrajit acknowledged his help. 'I am feeling better now. I just need some fresh air.' He got up and went outside the tent.

He searched around in the tents to see if he could find any of his men in the tents. 'Having them alive, even if injured, is all I want, Oh Lord,' he prayed as he kept searching. He could see injured Kalinga, Narayani and Chedi soldiers, but none of the Ustrakarnikas.

Hundreds of medics, charioteers and non-combatant infantry were pacing around to take injured soldiers into the tents, bring them from the battlefront, or take the dead bodies towards the camp outskirts. *If the war itself was a logistical nightmare, the arrangements made for food and medics must have been equally challenging,* he thought as he searched.

Even after searching for few minutes, he couldn't see any of the Ustrakarnikas. *May be whoever survived went to the camp site,* he thought and started going back to their tents.

All the while going back to the camp, Mitrajit prayed and wished to see as many of his men as possible. Once there, he went inside to find only Arochan, an injured Chitraangad, and Maarthanda, who was looking in better shape after freshening up.

Arochan looked at Mitrajit and moved his head side to side indicating no one else had returned. 'I don't know if there were others at the medic camp. How is Aparajit doing?'

Mitrajit looked down at the ground. Took a deep breath and replied, 'He is no more. We lost him and I have not seen any of our men at the medic camp. Maarthanda, can you stay with Chitraangad? You must be tired too and need to take some rest. Arochan, come along with me. We need to check for any information we can gather.'

Arochan followed Mitrajit out. Mitrajit went out to find most of the Narayani sena back at their camps. Very few Kalingas could be seen around.

They waited for four more ghadiyas in the hope that they may see someone from their tribe turn up. They searched around and also went to check in the medic camp again, but to no avail.

'What should we do now, Taatsri? It is getting late too.'

'I think we have to prepare for the inevitable, my son. It is better we check on the outskirts of the warzone and plan for the rituals,' Mitrajit replied as he remembered the steps Aparajit took the previous day.

As they were returning back from the medic camp, Mitrajit recognized General Satyavan from the Narayani sena. He was talking to his soldiers outside his tent. As Mitrajit went towards him to talk, the General saw Mitrajit approaching him and excused his soldiers to go ahead with their work.

'Ah. There you are, Mitrajit. I am sorry that we are meeting in this state. I was looking forward to our discussion at dinner today, but the circumstances have changed. So sorry for the losses your people have faced. Today was a tough day for all of us, including the Kalingas. But you all put up a brave fight. Aayusha came back from the medic camp, and he informed me that your leader Aparajit has succumbed to his injuries. I am so sorry for you to lose your leader. Please accept my condolences.'

'Thank you, General. I didn't expect to meet you in these circumstances. I came to ask a favor from you now that most of my men didn't return.'

'Please go ahead. Hope I can be of any assistance.'

'If you can, please guide and support me with the next steps. We were planning to go to the outskirts of the war zone to identify our people. Yesterday, Aparajit was there to do it, but today….,' Mitrajit couldn't stop his tears. It had been an emotional rollercoaster for the past few hours.

'Sorry,' Mitrajit continued wiping away his tears. 'But today I have to do it and I have no idea how.'

'I understand Mitrajit. I will send few of my men to escort you to the cremation site. They can help you with that.'

'I also wanted to ask you another favor. Aparajit wanted me to take whoever is left of us to Devasthana. It is very important now for us to go back and support the rest of our people. I don't know whom to connect with on this. I would have asked General Pattabhadra from the Kalingas, but he himself is in a state of shock.'

'Of course, Mitrajit. I don't think anyone from the Kaurava side will disagree with that request. Your people need the rest of you to support them. Let me connect with the Kaurava generals and confirm to you by dinner time if that is fine with you.'

'Thank you very much. I really appreciate your help.'

'You are welcome, Mitrajit. Now, let me send some of my men with you.'

General Satyavan went to talk to his men. He sent eight of his men with Mitrajit and Arochan to assist with the cremation rituals.

For the next few ghadiyas, Mitrajit and Arochan tried their best to identify their men. The whole area on the outskirts was filled with pyres for the thousands of soldiers who lost their life that day.

With a heavy heart, Mitrajit lit the fires on the pyres of Ustrakarnikas and broke into tears as he lit the special pyre for Aparajit. He looked around and the whole ground was lit by the flame-red light from the pyres. There were pyres seen on the Pandava side too on the western side of Kurukshetra, but they seemed to be lesser in number than on the Kaurava side, giving a clear indication whose side had lost the most on the second day.

'Pandavas may feel they won today, but did they really win if so many soldiers died on their side too? I don't know which side will eventually win this war, but I think everyone will lose a substantial number of their men by the end.' Arochan said as they both went back to the campsite.

'Yes. I only hope that all those brave soldiers who gave up their lives will not be forgotten. Though itihaasa[87] will remember the princes and kings from this war, I hope there will be a time when other soldiers will be acknowledged too.'

With heavy hearts, both came back to the campsite. Maarthanda saw them coming and not seeing anyone else with them, understood how grim the situation was. Seeing Arochan, he said, 'Chitra moved his head a bit. I think he is recovering. The medic came in a while ago to change the healing patches.'

'Ah. Some hope,' Arochan said as he went on to check his father.

Maarthanda came towards Mitrajit and said, 'So, looks like no one else survived.'

---

[87] History

Mitrajit slowly nodded while looking at Maarthanda.

'I can't process yet what has happened to us.'

'Me too, Maarthanda. It is a day Ustrakarnikas will never forget. I feel horrible that we couldn't even collect the ashes of our men. So many of them. There was no chance we could collect all of theirs. I only brought Aparajit's.'

'I understand, Mitra. He was like a father figure to all of us. Now, what do you think we should do now?'

'Well, before he took his last breath, Aparajit asked me to take the rest of us to Devasthana. I have reached out to General Satyavan of the Narayani sena to inquire if we can leave the war zone and head back home. He said that he will let us know later during dinner time. Let us go and check with him.'

At the dinner site, Satyavan could be seen talking with Pattabhadra. The General from Kalinga looked tired and sad from his expression. No surprise, as the General lost so many of his own men and leaders. Mitrajit couldn't imagine what must be going through Pattabhadra's mind. Losing their King and Prince! *How was their kingdom going to survive? How are we going to survive? And now without the Kalinga's support, how are we going to defend Devasthana against the Ekapaadas?* Mitrajit's thoughts came back to haunt him again.

Keeping his concerns aside, Mitrajit walked over to Satyavan and Pattabhadra.

'Good evening, Mitrajit. I was talking to General Pattabhadra here. I have also spoken with my commander, and we agreed that the one unit left from Kalinga army will be departing tomorrow back to their kingdom along with General Pattabhadra,' Satyavan said.

Mitrajit looked towards Pattabhadra with shock. Only one unit left of all thousands of soldiers making up an akshauhini. Pattabhadra was still looking down at the ground with a sad expression.

'You should also go back with them to your place,' Satyavan continued. 'I will send some of my men with you to provide you support during the journey and help in settling down things on your end. General Pattabhadra has explained to me the risk from the Ekapaadas for your people. Having our men may help a bit. The Ekapaadas may be cautious at the thought of attacking you when we are there to support you.'

Mitrajit looked at Pattabhadra, thankful to him for bringing up the Ekapaadas with Satyavan.

'My trusted lieutenant, Aayusha, who you already met, got slightly injured and I would want him to stay away from this war to heal. He and two other soldiers will accompany you on your journey,' Satyavan informed.

'Thank you for the information and the support, General. I also appreciate you sending some of your men with us. That is thoughtful. Now that the cremation rituals are done too, we will get our things packed up and if the medics give us a go ahead to take Chitraangad in the current state, we would like to join Pattabhadra's group at least till the Vindhyas before we head to Devasthana. Thanks again.'

'That works for us too, Mitrajit,' Pattabhadra finally joined the conversation. 'Let me know by morning as we are planning to start just after sunrise. It would be good to go together at least till the Vindhya mountains. Now, if you excuse me, I need to get back to my soldiers. Their morale is low, as you can imagine. See you in the morning. Please excuse me, Satyavan.'

'Of course. Go ahead, Pattabhadra. I will see you in the morning too,' Satyavan replied. After Pattabhadra left, he looked towards Mitrajit and asked, 'You look as if you have some other questions.'

'Well, so many questions General. But for now, I am curious to know if Aayusha is fine to come with us. I mean, accompanying us is one thing, but to stay and help us settle down may be another. I do not know how long that will take. I am happy that it's Aayusha, as I have understood him to be a bright and brave young man, but I just hope he is fine with being away from his own people for some time.'

'Not a problem at all. I have spoken to him, and he is fine with it too. Aayusha doesn't have anyone that he calls family. His family was killed in one of the attacks by King Jarasandha of Magadha back when we all Yadavas were still living in Mathura. He was open to the idea of joining you. When you feel that you are settled in, you can send him back to Dwarka. Hopefully by that time, this war will be over, and we will be in a better state to receive him in Dwarka.'

'Thanks, Satyavan. Appreciate all the help. Now please excuse me so that I can talk to my people.' Mitrajit paused. *What people?* he thought. *How many are left?*

He continued, 'Sorry, I meant Arochan and Maarthanda.'

'I understand your predicament Mitrajit, and I am sorry about that. I need to get going too. Aayusha will meet you in the morning, as he is resting now.'

'Thank you again,' Mitrajit said as Satyavan turned towards his units. Mitrajit took a deep breath before heading back to his tent.

Mitrajit saw Maarthanda lying down on his bed while Arochan sat beside Chitraangad's side with his head in his hands. Mitrajit could tell that the young man was still shocked at the events that had unfolded in front of him. *Who wouldn't be,* he thought. Arochan was already shocked at his father's condition, and today he was devastated by the loss of his friends. This day would be remembered for a long, long time.

'We cannot change what has already happened, son,' Mitrajit spoke as he sat beside the young man. 'We need to take your father and go back home. We got the permission from the commanders to leave whenever the medics gives a go ahead to take Chitra. We need to regroup and rebuild our city and the surrounding areas.'

Arochan looked at Mitrajit and said, 'How are we going to rebuild? With whom are we going to do that? Who is left to help us with it? Who are we without the rest of the men? We are done as Ustrakarnikas.'

Mitrajit looked at him and saw Arochan's red eyes with tears rolling down. Taking a deep breath Mitrajit replied. 'Let's be stronger, my son. We will make it through. Remember, we have families to take care of. Ustrakarnikas aren't just the men who fought in this war. Women, kids, and elders all make up our tribe too. We are not done yet. With the strong women and elders on our side we can help us Ustrakarnikas sustain into future generations.'

Arochan nodded slowly. He looked at Mitrajit and said, 'Yes, Taatsri. I will give my best to help our people survive through these tough times.'

'Good to hear, son.'

'Also, when you went to inquire with General Satyavan, the medic came in to said that pitashri's condition looks improving, and with the nutrition he is getting through the skin patches, he should recover well. The arm stump is healing well too, with no infection,' Arochan replied.

'Oh, that is good to hear.'

'You also need to get your shoulder checked, Taatsri.'

'It is better now, son. Now, why don't you go and have some dinner and take rest?'

'I am in no mood to have dinner now, Taatsri. I have lost my appetite.'

'I can understand, Arochan.'

That night was much quieter compared to previous nights; there weren't many men in the tents at their campsite, Mitrajit realized as he laid down on his bed.

9.Aavrutti[88] Parva

As Mitrajit got up to the sounds around him, he saw Arochan was already packing up.

'Good morning, I must have overslept. Let me get ready quickly,' Mitrajit said, feeling guilty.

'Good morning, Taatsri. I couldn't sleep well so I got up early and wanted to pack our things so that we could go whenever you were ready to have father checked up by the medics before they get busy,' Arochan said.

Before they get busy…. true, once the day's battles start, more injured soldiers will be added to the already high workload of the medics. Mitrajit thought.

---

[88] Return/ Returning

He saw Arochan's eyes were red and restless. The young man seemed to be struggling with everything happening around him. Mitrajit thought of talking to him further but decided to leave it out for the time being. Maybe during their journey back, he would have an opportunity and hopefully by that time Chitraangad would recover to bring some solace to the young man's anxiety. *He has lost so many of his friends. Just by seeing Chitraangad, if I am feeling in this way, I can't even imagine what must be going on in Arochan's mind,* Mitrajit thought.

Mitrajit freshened up quickly and started packing his stuff too. He saw Maarthanda placing all the men's stuff into one corner of the tent and went to help him.

'Do you need help to move them?' Mitrajit asked.

'I am good, thank you. I only wish we could take all of these items with us. The men brought their personal stuff, and I would hate to leave it all here,' Maarthanda said as he moved things to the corner.

'I wish too, Maarthanda. But you can imagine it will be tough for the three of us carry our stuff, Chitraangad and these many items. If we had carts that would have been useful.'

'I understand. It's just a wish.'

'I hear you. Let me know if you need a hand, otherwise we will go to the medic camp and come back.'

'You go ahead. I am almost done,' Maarthanda replied.

Mitrajit and Arochan put Chitraangad in a carrier and went out of the largely empty tent. The sky was still dark. *Hope the medics give good news so that we can leave by sunrise,* Mitrajit thought as they started heading towards the medic camp.

They met Aayusha on the way, who was heading towards their camp with two other men.

Seeing Mitrajit, Aayusha stopped and said, 'Good morning, Mitrajit. General Satyavan updated me about the plan. I am sorry about the huge losses your tribe have met with. Please accept my condolences. I am here with my two men, Shanthan and Chandra, who will accompany me on our journey with you. We are here at your service.'

'That is so kind of you to come and support us. Hope your injuries are better.'

'Oh, they're fine. Just a few cuts on the right arm and an arrow scraped through my left calf, nothing major. The medics have taken care of it already. I see that you are taking your friend to the medic camp. I will wait for you at your tent. If the medics are okay for you to leave, then we are ready to leave anytime.' Aayusha replied.

'Sure. Thank you. Yes, we are heading there and we can plan according to what the medics advise.' They continued to the medic tent.

'I would suggest you continue giving this medicine to him. Overall vital signs look to have stabilized. Keep changing these nutrition patches on his skin so that he can get energy supplied regularly and he may regain his consciousness soon. Make sure to keep changing bandages on the stump to avoid any infection. The stump will heal in a couple of days. If you can take care of these things, then I think you can go ahead with your plan of heading home,' the medic said.

'Absolutely. We will continue your advice. Thank you for everything and for giving us hope,' Arochan replied, excited to hear a positive prognosis from the medic.

Thanking the medics for their help and getting all the medication and bandages required, Mitrajit and Arochan headed back to the tent where General Pattabhadra was talking to Aayusha.

'Oh, there you are, Mitrajit. I was just checking with Aayusha to see if you were planning to join us for the journey back. We planned to leave as soon as the Kaurava allies take the formations for the day. Are the medics okay for Chitraangad to leave the camp yet?'

'Yes, Pattabhadra. Thanks for checking in with us. The medics looked very optimistic with Chitraangad's recovery and permitted us to travel today.'

'Good. We will move towards the eastern end of the campsite once the armies take the formations. Meet us there and we can start our journey back.'

'Sure. We should be ready by that time,' Mitrajit replied. He looked at Aayusha to check if he and his men were okay with the plan.

'We are ready too, General, and we will join you along with Mitrajit and the others,' Aayusha replied.

Mitrajit went in to see Maarthanda had already set their men's belongings to one side of the tent.

'We will be leaving as soon as the armies take today's formation, Maarthanda.' Mitrajit said and turned towards Aayusha and Arochan. 'It will take us two to three days to reach Devasthana if we can keep up a good pace. We have packed enough food. We can take turns to carry Chitraangad and hope that he gains consciousness soon. If he can walk, then we can pick up the face further.'

'Absolutely. I have checked that the forecast is for clear skies for the next few days. That should help with the journey too,' Aayusha replied.

'Oh, okay. Thank you.'

Their conversation was disturbed by the sounds of the conches and trumpets signaling the beginning of day three of the war. Mitrajit's thoughts came back to reality. All this while, he was engulfed in thinking about going back to Devasthana.

'There you go. Another day of fighting and killing to make the Kings and Princes happy. Many more wives to be widowed, and many more kids to be orphaned.' Arochan couldn't stop from expressing his anger and frustration.

'Don't say that, Arochan. I know you are disappointed by the way things have turned out. This is not what we wanted to happen, but let us not get bogged down with these thoughts anymore. We have the bigger responsibility now of taking care of our people. So, let us focus on that, my son,' Mitrajit replied.

'Sorry, Taatsri. I will not bring that up again. You are right, I should be focusing on building the right future for the rest of us.'

'That's good, Arochan. Now let us all pack our things and start moving.'

Mitrajit and others met General Pattabhadra at the eastern end of the war camp. Pattabhadra saw Mitrajit looking at Kalinga soldiers lining up for the journey and said, 'Only one hundred and fifteen of us left, Mitrajit. That's what our fate has been.'

Mitrajit looked at the General in surprise. *A whole akshauhini wiped out in a matter of two days,* he thought. 'That is a huge loss for you too, Pattabhadra. I am so sorry.'

'Well, it is what it is, Mitrajit. Our hope is to go home and then regroup. We will then assess what our next steps could be. If the Kauravas win this war and King Karna is still victorious, I hope and wish for the Anga kingdom to support us. Anyways, all we can do is hope and pray.'

Mitrajit nodded in agreement. All they could do too was hope and pray.

Pattabhadra turned to his men and signaled them to keep moving. Mitrajit, along with Arochan and Maarthanda, carrying Chitraangad, followed behind the General with Aayusha and his men behind them.

Though they were moving towards the south away from the camp site, they all kept an eye on the warfront. Dust started filling up the sky while the rain of arrows made some areas of the sky go darker. They could hear the battle cries and the thunderous sounds of the advanced weapons. They could feel the earth vibrate below them from the movement of the chariots. The battle sounds were reverberating across the warzone.

As they moved away from the warzone, Mitrajit noticed that the observers, whom he saw the previous day, were still on the small hillocks writing their observations. *I hope someone will write about the sacrifices our tribe made in the observations they're making,* Mitrajit thought as they walked along the passes around the hills to go further south of Kurukshetra.

The sounds became fainter as they moved away. 'It is interesting to see how most of the villages on the way look deserted,' Maarthanda pointed out as they crossed many small villages on their way towards Hastinapura.

'I hope that at least the men from these villages can come back safely,' Arochan expressed.

Mitrajit couldn't disagree with that statement. He wished for the same in his mind.

Oh, what all did I wish for and what has happened? How do I tell everyone back home? How will the rest of us Ustrakarnikas survive? Will the Ekapaadas attack now if they know that most of our men were killed? Will we be able to defend them? How can the Kalingas help them now that even they are very few?' So many questions were popping up in Mitrajit's mind as they kept moving.

'If we can keep up this pace, we can reach Kausambi by evening. We can camp there for the night,' General Pattabhadra's announcement brought Mitrajit back from his thoughts. *Good pace, of course,* he thought. Everyone wanted to reach home as soon as possible.

'Good to know. Meanwhile, I wanted to ask….' Mitrajit was just about to complete his sentence when Pattabhadra intervened.

'Is this about the continuance of our alliance, Mitrajit?'

Surprised by Pattabhadra's words, Mitrajit said, 'Yes, how did you know I was planning to ask that?'

'It was obvious, Mitrajit. You looked lost in your thoughts as we passed Hastinapura.'

Mitrajit felt guilty, 'Sorry, I was. I hope you can understand.'

'Of course, my friend. I am also in the same boat as you. Not even in my worst nightmare would I have thought of losing our King, our Prince and so many of our brave men, until we are now only a hundred left. But I know we will be able to regroup. One thing is for sure: our King's promise is our promise. We will respect that and continue our friendship and alliance. Even with our limited capacity, we will be there to support you at any time you need.'

Hearing the reassuring words, Mitrajit replied, 'I really appreciate those words, Pattabhadra. I respect that even while going through all these difficulties yourself, you and the Kalingas are still willing to help us. I sincerely thank you.'

'Oh, don't say that, Mitrajit. We are friends now. We are all together in this.'

*****

After crossing Kausambi by evening, Pattabhadra signaled everyone to camp for the night. Mitrajit took the opportunity to meditate before having dinner. The scenes from the battlefield kept flashing in front him as he tried his best to calm himself down to meditate. Unable to meditate further, he went to meet others for dinner.

As he sat down to eat, Arochan shouted, 'Taatsri, come here. Pitashri is moving and trying to open his eyes.'

Mitrajit was excited to hear that. He immediately got up and went to Chitraangad's side to see his friend struggling to keep his eyes open. Mitrajit went closer to him and held his left hand. 'Chitra. This is Mitrajit. Can you hear me?'

Chitraangad nodded slightly and looked around to see Mitrajit and Arochan sitting on either side of him. He looked confused as to where he was and turned towards Mitrajit to ask. He tried to talk, but was too weak to move his lips.

'It's okay, Chitra. Have some water.' He lifted Chitraangad's head a bit to make it easy to take a sip of water from the leather pouch.

Chitraangad took few sips of water and asked with a faint voice, 'What happened? Where are we?'

Mitrajit took a deep breath and said, 'You were hurt in the battle, Chitra, and lost a lot of blood. You were unconscious for a couple of days. We are on our way back to Devasthana. Glad to see you awake, my friend.'

Chitraangad seemed to realize something and looked at his right arm. It was heavily bandaged on the stump just above his elbow. He gave a concerned look towards Arochan and Mitrajit.

'Don't worry, pitashri. Glad you are alive and conscious. You fought bravely.' Arochan was putting on a brave face as he tried to give confidence to his father.

Chitraangad looked at Mitrajit and inquired, 'Why are we heading back? Did the war end? Did we defeat the Pandavas? Where is everyone?' He looked around, finding no other Ustrakarnikas except for Maarthanda.

Mitrajit looked into Chitraangad's eyes and said, 'The war is not over, Chitra, but there is a lot you need to be updated about.' Mitrajit then went on to inform Chitraangad on the events of the past two days.

Chitraangad was shocked to hear about the losses they had and was devastated by Aparajit's demise. 'This is a sad thing for all of us. So many killed in just a day, and how many more by the end of this war? I am glad the few of us have been allowed to leave and escape that madness. I always wanted to fight and show our skills, but this war was on a different scale. We should not have been at this war.'

'I agree with you, my friend,' Mitrajit continued, 'but right now, don't worry about anything else and take some rest. We will continue on our journey and try to reach Devasthana sooner.'

Arochan then changed the bandages and applied medicine to Chitraangad's arm stump. 'Once you start eating food, you can slowly regain your energy too, pitashri,' he said as he fed Chitraangad the food they packed.

Tears rolled from Chitraangad's eyes, looking at his son feeding him. 'I never thought a day like this would come when my son, whom I used to feed as a child, is now feeding me,' he said.

'Never say that, pitashri. I am just glad that you are alive. This is nothing compared to all you have done for me. Now, please eat,' Arochan said as he wiped Chitraangad's tears.

That night Mitrajit went to sleep with mixed feelings. He was happy that they were out of that warzone, his friend was regaining his consciousness, and that he would be seeing Dhruti and Purna soon. At the same time, he was agonizing over how to communicate the news with the women, kids and elders back at Devasthana. He was also worried at how everyone would take the news. The physical effort from the day's walking while carrying Chitraangad's carrier slowly helped him fall asleep.

The next morning, Chitraangad looked to be in better shape. He was able to walk with his arm around Arochan. They all took turns to support Chitraangad while he on their journey.

When it was Mitrajit's turn to support Chitraangad, he took the opportunity and said, 'I am sorry, Chitra. I think you got distracted during the battle because of me and that got your concentration away from your fight,' Mitrajit started expressing his guilt at the way the incident unfolded.

'No, no. Don't say that!' Chitraangad cut Mitrajit short. 'My gaze just fell on you, that is all. I was keeping an eye on Arochan too just to make sure he was safe too. I think it's my old age that made me respond slowly. You, my friend, could never cause harm to me. Moreover, you helped me survive by being there to take me to the medics.'.

Mitrajit felt better after getting some reassurance from Chitraangad.

Chitraangad continued, 'But there is one thing I am worried about now, Mitra. I am concerned as to how Subhadra will react looking at my condition.'

'Well, I think Subhadra will be shocked at first, but at the same time, I think she will understand the situation. Seeing you and Arochan both being alive and safe itself will be the most important thing for her.'

'True, Mitra. I am being selfish on my end in thinking of only how my wife would react to my situation when it is actually mine and your family who are the lucky ones in the village. I cannot even fathom how others will take the news.'

'Well, it is what it is, Chitra. It has been stressing me too, wondering how it may all turn out back in Devasthana.'

'One step at a time, Aparajit would say. So, let us see how it all evolves once we start informing them. We need to be strong to guide the village back on its feet. I think once we go and communicate the message, we will also get an idea on what everyone wants. We can then plan on our next steps of consolidating whoever is left in Devasthana.'

Mitrajit was so happy to see his friend getting back to consciousness and being there to support him. He always felt that Chitraangad would step up to be the head of the tribe when Aparajit would be too old to continue. Instead, ever since Aparajit asked him to become the chief, he has been feeling burdened by that thought.

'Thanks, Chitra, for the suggestion and support. I am so glad that you are up and back. Now I can be relaxed. But, I have been wanting to ask you something. I want you head our tribe. Aparajit gave that responsibility to me before he passed away, but that could be because you were unconscious. I always felt that you would be the right heir for taking over that position. All the other Ustrakarnikas also see you as their next leader.'

Chitraangad looked at his friend and smiled. 'Oh, Mitra. I can understand why Aparajit must have taken this decision. It is not just because I was unconscious but also because he knows that you are more levelheaded than me. You know how I can get too excited in some situations and make rash decisions. Look at this war itself; I was so excited to get into the war and show our strength and fighting skills. But see how it turned out to be for me and our people? Devasthana doesn't need a chieftain who just has experience, but they need someone who has been a long-standing leader while also being wise and controlled in his thoughts. Aparajit was right with his choice. I am so happy for this, and I will always be there to support you. Now don't hesitate anymore and no more questions about this. You gave a promise to Aparajit and let us respect the old man's wish.' Chitraangad hugged his friend as he said that, both to reassure him and to show his affection for their friendship.

Mitrajit's eyes swelled with tears. He could always count on Chitraangad.

'Friends forever, brothers always,' Mitrajit said as he returned his hug. With his friend, and Dhruti and Purna by his side, he felt confident to pass through these tough times.

With Chitraangad able to walk again, the journey heading back became easier. They reached the boundaries of Nishada kingdom by evening and continued south towards the Vindhyas.

Just before nightfall, Mitrajit noticed that there was a commotion among the Kalinga group. Arochan went to check and came back to inform them that the Kalinga messengers were on their way back as part of their routine. 'The messengers were shocked at the news and are now going to head back to their kingdom with their group.'

'Let us check if they have any news from our people,' Mitrajit said.

'I am sorry to hear about the loss of your men and your leader,' the messenger said, looking at Mitrajit. General Pattabhadra was also there standing beside his messengers.

'The news from Devasthana is that they took no news as good news, but we were told by Lady Kumudini that most of the families in Devasthana and other villages were planning to stay or leave depending on the outcome. She wanted to ensure that Aparajit was informed of this so that he can plan accordingly when you all would head back,' the messenger updated, looking down while saying the last sentence.

'Thank you, I appreciate the condolences offered and for the news you have for us.' Mitrajit thanked the messenger.

General Pattabhadra came beside Mitrajit and said, 'My friend, we decided that we will be heading east tomorrow morning instead of going up to the training camp as we planned to inform our people from other villages on the way to our home. With so few of us left, it may be difficult to send the message across the kingdom. This way we will at least reach some of the villages on our way.'

'Good idea, Pattabhadra. We may also plan something like that,' Mitrajit replied.

'But one thing I would like to promise is that we will always respect your allegiance.'

'I appreciate your confirmation and definitely look forward to our continued communication, General. Let us also know if we can be of any help to you.' Mitrajit was hesitant while speaking that sentence, but he wanted to make sure he offered their support too.

'Of course, Mitra. Thanks for the offer. This is the reason why we appreciate you Ustrakarnikas. Your hearts are so big. Even in these difficult times, you are offering your help. Thanks again,' General Pattabhadra replied while putting his hand on his heart, showing his thankfulness.

The next day morning, Pattabhadra came to say goodbye to Mitrajit and Chitraangad. 'It is good to see you recovering well, Chitraangad,' he said. 'It was a pleasure meeting you both. I hope that we can connect again soon.'

Mitrajit and Chitraangad both nodded in agreement. After the Kalinga troops and Pattabhadra left towards east, Mitrajit and the others continued their southward journey towards Devasthana.

Arochan followed up regularly to rub the medicinal balms on his father's arm stump to minimize any infections, and continuously changed his bandages.

Now that they were a smaller group Mitrajit and others were able to pace themselves quicker. They reached the deserted training camp before lunch time. *Just a few days back, the site was abuzz with soldiers and all of them were enjoying the feast that was arranged by King Srutayush of the Kalingas,* Mitrajit thought as they had their lunch.

*****

As they were having lunch, Chitraangad asked Aayusha, 'How is to live on an island?' Being inland in the Bharata varsha it was an interesting thought for him that the Yadavas live on an island in Dwarka.

'Oh, it has its advantages and disadvantages,' Aayusha replied. He looked around and saw there was interest among Mitrajit and Arochan too.

'You get to eat a lot of fish being surrounded by the Paschim saagara[89]. You must have eaten fish from the lakes, but the fish from the sea are much better in my opinion.' Shanthan and Chandra, the other Yadavas accompanying them nodded in agreement with Aayusha's reply.

---

[89] Current Arabian Sea

'Dwarka is made up of many islands,' Aayusha continued. 'Our royalty lives on the main island while others live on surrounding islands. I live on the shankhodara[90] dweep[91]. We use boats to come to the mainland. The port is heavily guarded, and a draw gate is the only way to get into each of these islands. The only people allowed to enter are the ones with a Yadava kingdom's permit with their seal on it. I felt safer living in Dwarka than in Mathura.' Aayusha's face looked grim as he mentioned that.

Mitrajit remembered General Satyavan telling him about how Aayusha's parents and brother were killed during King Jarasandha's attacks. He also reminisced how at one of their regular meetings at Devasthana, Aparajit mentioned the news of how whole population of the Yadava kingdom moved and settled down near the sea on the west coast. It was something they had never heard of happening before in Bharata varsha. Kings would fight to win or lose their kingdoms but to move onto a different part of the region was never done before.

Even though everyone was appreciative of Krishna's strengths as a warrior, commander, and diplomat, it was surprising that he chose that route. Interestingly, his brother Balarama also agreed, as no one would have messed with him if he wanted to fight.

The Yadava clan could have easily won against Jarasandha, Mitrajit thought. But just like Ustrakarnikas being attacked regularly by the

---

[90] In shape of Conch/Shell

[91] Island

Ekapaadas, even the Yadavas were tired of being attacked by the Magadha armies. The small but quick units of the Magadha army would attack Mathura repeatedly, causing more panic and damage than a full-fledged war. Many civilians were killed in those relentless attacks, including Aayusha's parents.

'Yes, of course, I remember Krishna moving the whole Yadava kingdom to Dwarka,' Chitraangad said as Aayusha stopped explaining about Dwarka. 'We also discussed on how we could end the skirmishes with the Ekapaadas. At that time Mitra suggested that we take cues from the Yadavas and move Ustrakarnikas to somewhere north of Vindhyas. But Aparajit and the other elders were not convinced at that time. Aparajit felt that we were not as mighty or rich as the Yadava kingdom to get land anywhere they wanted. Hence it was decided to look for alliances with stronger kingdoms like the Kalingas.'

'Well, it would not have made any difference for us as we would still be drawn into this war, and we would have ended up in the same situation anyways.' Mitrajit replied.

'True. We never know how and where our fate will take us, my friend,' Chitraangad said. Everyone nodded in agreement.

The next two days of the journey were uneventful. The journey helped Arochan to slowly come out of the throes of the battlefield. He was able to connect with the other young Yadava young men. Arochan was in awe of the rigorous physical and mental programs that the Narayani sena had to undergo as part of their military training.

'It is important for a warrior to understand that he is going to take a life in a battle if needed and that is part of his role. Otherwise it's you who will be killed. Hence, we are trained on how to cope up with the thought of killing and fighting,' Aayusha explained.

'That is so important. I have been feeling stressed and anxious whenever I would recall the events at the war. I am happy that I survived but sad to kill so many soldiers too. I wish we had similar training too,' Arochan replied.

Mitrajit along with Chitraangad and Maarthanda kept up the pace with the youngsters.

'We would have been in better position if King Karna participated from the beginning of this war,' Chitraangad mentioned.

'We will never know how it could have turned out. The fate of this war was already decided by the Gods, and I don't know how Karna's participation would have helped,' Maarthanda replied.

'True. We will never know. But one thing we can try to do is get back safely and rebuild,' Mitrajit said. 'Though I am curious what must be happening right now at Kurukshetra. Hope we will get some news soon.'

*****

As they were closing in towards the first of their twelve villages, Ramapura, Arochan expressed his concern. 'I can't imagine how we will deliver the devastating news and I don't know how everyone will react to it.'

Chitraangad said, 'Let us be strong, my son. It is inevitable. Me and Mitrajit will try our best to tell them'.

At the outskirts of Ramapura, they saw kids playing with sticks re-enacting a battle scene. The kids stopped playing when they saw Mitrajit and others in the soldier's outfit. Mitrajit told them to go and inform Vali, one of the elders, that he would like to talk to all the villagers and to gather everyone at the mound on the outskirts of the village.

Within minutes, elders, women, and kids started gathering around the mound. There was a commotion among them as everyone wanted to get the news and were eager to hear why only a few of the soldiers were back.

Once he felt there was enough of a gathering, Mitrajit took a deep breath and announced. 'I am deeply sorry to convey this news to you, but many of our brave men lost their lives in the battles of Kurukshetra. Everyone representing your village died fighting valiantly in the war. We have completed their funeral with all necessary respected rituals. We have also lost our leader Aparajit. We are the only ones left from the entire Ustrakarnikas army that went to fight.'

Immediately, they could hear people gasping, shouting, crying, and screaming questions. Mitrajit looked at Chitraangad with a worried look. They were never in a position like this before.

Chitraangad understood the challenge of his friend. He came forward to support him. Looking at the crowd, he raised his left hand up and waived to gain attention.

'Everyone, listen,' Chitraangad continued. 'I know it is not the news you all wanted to hear. But with Aparajit gone, we all must trust our new leader, Mitrajit. We are going to head to Devasthana and plan on our next steps and will convey further information to you all.'

Mitrajit looked around to see everyone crying or surprised at the news they just heard. He doubted if anyone even heard Chitraangad's words.

'What all you did you leaders bring upon to us? What should we do now without our men? How can we be assured we will be safe from the Ekapaadas? It's better we move away from here,' an elder from the crowd shouted.

More people followed him and started shouting.

'I am leaving today out of this village.'

'Me too. Enough of this farce with the war and carnage.'

'There is nothing left for me.'

'You leaders unnecessarily dragged all of us into this war.'

'I understand your situation. I will plan to ensure we will restore peace,' Mitrajit tried to be heard above the commotion from the crowd.

'To hell with your peace. I am going out of this village.'

'Please help us. We are too old to do anything for my family.'

'I will leave with my kids to my ancestor's place in Pulinda'.

Mitrajit was perplexed at the responses he got from the crowd. Some of them started moving away from them towards their houses, while others sat down near the mound, crying and shouting.

Chitraangad whispered to Mitrajit, 'Looks like they are not in a position to understand our assurances now, Mitra. We may have to come back later,' he said.

"Let's get out of here. They're not in a position to understand what you are trying to say. They are not even listening. Let us talk to Vali and hopefully he can communicate with the rest of the villagers once the crowd settles down,' Maarthanda suggested.

'Good idea. Let's keep going. Maarthanda, can you tell Vali that we will be coming back with our plans and until then to try to placate everyone?' Mitrajit asked.

'Of course. You go ahead, and I will catch up with you.'

Mitrajit informed the others and they went around the village to the southern side and waited for Maarthanda.

Maarthanda came just behind them. 'Vali was also in no mood to listen to us. I had no other choice but to leave them for now.'

'Understood. Thanks for trying, Maarthanda.' He felt bad that he himself stayed away from the crowd. That was not how he wanted to be portrayed as a leader of this group.

'This is going to be tough. If this is the reaction from Ramapura people, then I don't know how other villages and our own Devasthana people will receive the news.' Maarthanda said.

Everyone looked at each other with concern.

'You did what you could. This is not easy to take in news like this. Let's continue,' Aayusha reminded him about the task ahead.

Within the next ghadiya, they reached the outskirts of Devasthana. Mitrajit felt excited at the thought of seeing Dhruti and

Purna again. They would be so happy to see him alive and safe, he knew. At the same time, he was angry with himself of thinking selfishly about his family and their reaction when there were thousands of others who would have to receive bad news. His nervousness increased as they closed in on the village.

Chitraangad covered his arm stump with his angavastram[92]. 'I don't want Subhadra to see me in this state first. It will be way easier to explain it to her later,' he said to Arochan.

'They are here. They are back. Arochan is back.' Someone from the village saw them and shouted. Some ran towards the village to inform the rest.

Everyone started rushing out of their homes onto the roads with excitement. As soon as they saw Mitrajit and Chitraangad with only a couple of others behind them, they slowed down with a concerned look on their faces.

The women and elders were getting anxious and started asking questions.

What happened?'

Where are others? Where is our leader, Aparajit?'

Why don't you answer?'

Where is my son, Angad?'

Where is my husband, Dharmasena? Why is he not with you?'

---

[92] Cloth worn on torso

10. Bhaisajya[93] Parva

Mitrajit and Chitraangad moved on towards the center of the village while trying to avoid answering individually. *It is better to address them together,* Mitrajit thought. Dhruti and Purna came running along and hugged Mitrajit. Mitrajit was so happy to see them, though he was not able to express his excitement. The incident in Ramapura and now facing the villagers' questions made it awkward for him to show his excitement.

'Glad to see you back, pitashri. Did the war finish already? Did we win? Where are others?' Purna already started asking questions with innocence radiating from her face.

---

[93] Healing

Mitrajit looked at her then looked down with a defeated look on his face. Purna immediately understood that something must be wrong. She never saw her father react to her questions that way. She stopped asking questions and hugged her father. Her father could not lose. He was always a champion for her. She couldn't see the disappointment on his face. 'It is okay, pitashri. Glad to have you come back,' she said.

Mitrajit felt the warm hug and was thankful for having a daughter who was so understanding. He looked up to see all the villagers who were gathering around and turning impatient. There were elders, women and kids eagerly waiting for him or Chitraangad to answer their questions.

Subhadra came running and saw Chitraangad and Arochan. She was so happy and hugged them. Suddenly, she took a step back and looked at Chitraangad in shock. She couldn't feel his right arm!

Chitraangad removed the cloth he had put on top of him and showed his arm stump with bandages. 'Don't worry, Subhadra. Except for this, I am safe. This was an unfortunate incident,' he said while looking at Mitrajit as an indication that it was time that he should address the villagers.

Mitrajit stood on the platform of the village's chatvaram and raised his hand to calm down everyone. He could see Kumudini in front of the crowd. She looked at him and he could sense that she already understood what was going on. She must have guessed why Mitrajit is standing to address and why there was no sight of Aparajit. She did put on a brave face. *Maybe she is hoping to hear the news that her husband is still safe at the Kurukshetra war,* Mitrajit thought. In a minute, the whole place had gone quiet.

'My dear fellow Ustrakarnikas, I am here to say that we fought in one of the toughest wars Bharata varsha has ever seen. I am sad to say that except for a few of us, none of the other Ustrakarnikas has survived the war. On the second day of the battle, all our warriors were killed by Bheema and his army. Even most of the Kalinga army units were decimated. Our leader Aparajit has also succumbed to his injuries,'

Mitrajit looked at Kumudini at that point and continued with the announcement. He could see tears rolling down from her eyes.

'Aparajit wanted me to lead you all. Chitraangad and I will do our best to support you all. We will be connecting with some of the elders tomorrow morning, and we will chalk out a plan. The remaining Kalinga army and their general promised to continue their support to us. We are also joined by these warriors from Krishna's Narayani sena who are here to help us during these troubled times,' Mitrajit said while pointing towards Aayusha and his two soldiers.

Mitrajit took a pause to gauge the mood but immediately realized that it was a mistake. As soon as he paused, the gathered crowd became emotional and started crying. Some of them collapsed right there in a state of shock. Dhruti looked at Mitrajit with concern. She was happy that her husband came back, but the rest of the women were not that lucky. Almost all the women she knew and grew up with in the village had lost their husband, brother, or son.

Mitrajit understood the concerned look of Dhruti, but he was now the leader of the tribe, and he had to step up. With the crowd now broken down by their emotions, Mitrajit raised his voice again to console and provide confidence in the next steps being taken. 'I am sorry for your loss. I have personally ensured that the last cremation rituals were done with highest of honors for them. I can assure you that we will plan our way forward to ensure a brighter future for our tribe. All I need is support and patience as we move forward.'

No one seemed to be interested in listening him. *Who would be in a state to listen to me while I've just delivered such devastating news?* he thought. He got down from the platform and was met by Dhruti and Purna.

'Don't get stressed by what you see around, swami. You know it is tough news for everyone. Let them recover from this and we can connect with them tomorrow morning.' Dhruti was as supportive as she always had been.

'She's right,' Chitraangad chipped in. 'We better let them digest the news. Let them also plan on what they would like to do. I will let Arochan get some rest before he can communicate with other villages too.'

Chitraangad looked at Subhadra who was still in a shock from knowing that Chitraangad lost his arm and said, 'Don't worry, dear. I am fine. My wound is healing, and I have you to support me. The villagers need all the help. You should be with Kumudini during the toughest times for her.' Subhadra slowly nodded.

Dhruti and Subhadra went to console Kumudini who was kneeling on the ground and crying. Chitraangad's heart was pounding at the sight of that. Ever since he lost his father, Aparajit and Kumudini had supported him like his own parents. Now to see her in that state was heart wrenching for him.

Arochan looked at Aayusha and said, 'If you don't mind, we should be going so that I can show you the guest rooms for you to stay in, as I would like to come back and check on the parents of my friends.'

Aayusha nodded and looked at Mitrajit to inform him.

'Please go ahead Aayusha,' Mitrajit said. 'You and your soldiers need to rest. We have some real long days to look forward to.'

Meanwhile, Dhruti and Subhadra accompanied Kumudini to her home. They tried their best to keep up a brave face in front of her. Kumudini was inconsolable for some time before she took a deep breath and said, 'This is it. There is no one else for me here. I will go back to my brother's place.' Dhruti and Subhadra didn't say a word. They were not sure how to convince her to stay. Kumudini lost her husband, the only person through whom she had any connection to Devasthana.

After everyone started leaving the chatvaram, Mitrajit along with Purna started walking towards their home. Mitrajit looked at Purna. How dearly he had missed her and Dhruti. On one hand, he was happy to see them again and being safe, but his heart was aching from the wails and questions he could hear from the crowd behind him. *So many villages and kingdoms across the Bharata varsha will be crying out for their lost sons,* he thought. If two days of battles caused such damage to them and to the Kalingas, it cannot be imagined how the current situation would be with the war still raging.

*****

Once home, Mitrajit went towards the well to take a quick shower. He didn't even realize how cold the water was as his thoughts were still fixated on the next steps. *What would Aparajit do in this situation?* He would take steps to ensure everyone felt safe. Mitrajit had to look at providing confidence to everyone that they would be safe in Devasthana. *But with very few of us, how can I do that?* He was brought back to the reality when he heard Dhruti talking to Purna. She must have come back after meeting Kumudini, Mitrajit guessed.

By the time Mitrajit went in, Dhruti placed mats and plates on the ground for dinner. 'I am not in a mood to eat now, Dhruti,' Mitrajit said.

'I understand, swami. But we all need you to be stronger so that you can take care of the whole tribe properly.'

Mitrajit looked at her and nodded. 'Yes, you are right,' he said as he sat down. 'Where is Purna? She came along with me to home from the chatvaram.'

'She went to check on with her friends Bhumi and Suvarna. Poor girl, she seemed happy that you came back alive but at the same time devastated with the news and was feeling sorry for her friends.'

Mitrajit took a deep breath and said, 'She is a very understanding girl. I am glad she wanted to check on her friends.'

That evening before going to bed, Mitrajit updated both Dhruti and Purna on the events at the warfront, along with the reactions they received at Ramapura. They both took time to sink in the information.

'I feel myself to be extremely lucky and thankful to Lord Shiva for having you come back safely, pitashri. Not everyone was so lucky. So many of my friends lost their fathers,' Purna said as she gave a long hug to Mitrajit.

'Yes, we are very lucky, dear. We need to be thankful to Lord Shiva. We should now support our villagers to help them through these tough times.'

'Yes, pitashri.' Purna felt good after the long hug.

That night, the thoughts of the war, the sight of dead bodies of his fellow Ustrakarnikas, and the emotional responses from the villagers kept bothering Mitrajit and made it difficult for him to sleep.

Dhruti was not able to sleep either. It was hard for her to digest the fact that so many villagers had lost their lives. Her husband could have been one of them too. *Thanks to thathaastu devatas,* she thought. They did listen to her prayers and wishes. But not everyone was that lucky. They both could still hear the wailing sounds from the houses nearby.

Slowly fatigue overcame Mitrajit, and he went into a deep state of sleep. He dreamt of a chariot coming and taking him, Dhruti and Purna to the top of the mountain. Below, the valley seemed to be filled with dead bodies. As the chariot was about to reach the top, Mitrajit slipped and fell down into the valley.

'Please hold on to me, Dhruti, I don't want to die,' he murmured under his breath as he felt himself being pulled into the valley. He suddenly opened his eyes and saw Dhruti sitting beside him, holding his hand. 'You were dreaming, swami. Don't worry anymore. You are home and safe now,' she said.

Mitrajit wiped off the sweat on his forehead and took a sip of water. He then lied down while Dhruti slowly caressed his hair. He was able to slowly get back to sleep.

*****

As soon as he woke up in the morning, Mitrajit freshened up quickly and said to Dhruti, 'I have to go and connect with Chitraangad. We need to plan on the next steps.'

On any other day, Dhruti would have stopped him and asked him to have breakfast before he went out. But not today. She herself was longing to go and visit Kumudini.

As Mitrajit went out towards Chitraangad's house, he saw some families were packing and some of them were already leaving their houses with bags and carts. He was overwhelmed to see so many of them leaving. Were they not confident in him to take care of them? He had promised Aparajit that he would be there for the rest of the Ustrakarnikas, but it looked like most of them had already decided to leave even before hearing him out.

He asked the elderly Hari on the way who was leaving with his daughter in-law and grandson. 'Uncle, what happened? Where are you all going?'

'Well, there is nothing left for us here, Mitra. I am taking my daughter in-law to her parents in the west. It will be better for her to be with her parents. I don't know when I will have to leave this body and reach vaikuntam[94]. I will live my rest of my life with my grandson too,' Hari replied as they kept on walking.

Mitrajit looked at Hari and bowed down with a pranam[95]. 'May you have a safe journey and do remember to reach out to us if you need assistance at any point,' Mitrajit said. He couldn't muster enough energy to convince Hari and his family to stay back. He looked around to see much of the village packing up and leaving. 'How could he stop everyone? What was left for most of them to stay at this village?' he wondered as he reached Chitraangad's house.

Chitraangad was sitting in the verandah of his house with Arochan and Aayusha beside him. As soon as he saw Mitrajit, Chitraangad said, 'You must have seen the madness that has crept into the villager's heads. How can they leave the village and go? Wasn't this the same village that they all grew in and lived with their husbands and sons? Why would they leave?' Chitraangad seemed to be taken aback by the way the villagers had taken the shocking news from the war.

---

[94] God's abode

[95] Salutation

Mitrajit looked at his friend and shrugged. 'Well, there is nothing we can do now. Maybe we need to understand that every individual wants to protect their own. They all know that it will take a long time for us all to settle down, and who knows what the future may bring. Yes, the rest of us can support them, but no one is closer to them than their own families. Maybe I would have been okay with Dhruti and Purna going to Keertipuram if anything happened to me,' Mitrajit tried to put some context to the villagers leaving them.

'Of course, who am I to say these things? We are not in their position to understand their sentiments. We are the lucky ones to come out of that war in person, though injured. I mean, I am still alive with my son beside me and my best friend with me,' Chitraangad replied.

Mitrajit nodded in agreement. He then looked at Arochan and asked him to go with Aayusha and check how many from Devasthana had already left or were planning to leave. It was important to understand how many of them wanted to leave so that they could start to plan the next steps.

He sat down with Chitraangad and said 'I am planning to send message across the region to all our villages and invite them to move to Devasthana so that we can consolidate with whoever wants to stay. That way we can make Devasthana sustainable and hopefully keep our culture and heritage intact. We may have few men left, but we have so many boys who can grow up here and we can teach them all the necessary skills to grow up into the next generation of Ustrakarnikas. The elderly can teach them the puranas[96] and vedas[97].'

'Couldn't agree more, Mitra. Good idea.' Chitraangad replied. 'It should be shared with everyone else as soon as possible. Arochan along with Aayusha can go around to the remaining villages and convey the message. Hope everyone will have confidence and come over to join us here. It will also help us gather enough people to defend Devasthana in case the Ekapaadas seek to attack at this time.'

Mitrajit looked at his friend and smiled. 'Thanks for your confidence in the plan, Chitra. Yes, that was the reason I was thinking we should all be together. It will be tough to defend individual villages too. Let us hope for the best. By the way, how is Subhadra today?' he asked, curious to know how she was reacting to seeing her husband injured.

'Well, no complaints, Mitra. She understood and expressed her happiness for having me back alive along with Arochan. I think seeing at what's happened, she feels herself as the luckiest woman on earth now. She is concerned about Kumudini and everyone else. She left in the morning to meet her.'

Mitrajit nodded. 'Yeah. Can't imagine what is going through her mind now. I sincerely hope she stays back. It will be a good message to give confidence to other villagers. I don't know what updates Arochan might come back with.'

---

[96] Historical scriptures

[97] Religious scriptures

That afternoon, Arochan came back with grim news. 'Except for six families, rest are planning to leave. Hari and his family already left, and Vamsi and his. Most of them are packing and may leave by end of today or tomorrow morning. With Aparajit's death and with most of our people lost, the villagers feel there is not much they can do by staying back here. I tried to explain that we will be coming up with the plans soon. Did you both come up with something?' he asked.

'Well, it is sad to hear that they don't want to stay. We both thought that with so few of us left the only way we could sustain and also survive if Ekapaadas attack is to live together in Devasthana. The defenses are better here and with so many families leaving us, there are so many empty houses that others can move in. Of course, this all depends on how many of them would like to move and stay here,' Mitrajit replied.

'Here is an announcement, I wrote it down on the palm leaf,' he continued. 'Now if you and Aayusha can deliver it to the rest of the villages, they can have a chance to know our plan and think what the best step for them could be. You and Aayusha can leave after lunch and try to get the message as soon as possible,' Mitrajit looked at Aayusha as he said those words to check if he would be comfortable to do so.

Aayusha nodded to show his agreement.

'Devasthana would have come across as a vibrant village at any other time, Aayusha. Sad we couldn't show you how it would have been in normal times,' Mitrajit said.

'Oh no, I understand. These are not ordinary times. Even Dwarka wasn't recognizable after the many attacks by King Shalwa on his Saubha vimana[98]. Do not worry. I know that your culture will be sustained just as we Yadavas have survived. I wish you all the best in your plans. I am happy to go with Arochan and give them the confidence and share my own experiences if needed. Hopefully, I will be able to convince at least a few of them to join you all at Devasthana. I understand it is very important to have more than a few families here.' Aayusha replied.

'Thanks for the understanding. Let us all have hope that they all will join us. Aparajit was our leader for the past few decades. It will be hard for them to trust me.' Mitrajit was still not convinced that his words and plans would be taken seriously by the rest of the Ustrakarnikas.

'Not your fault, Mitra. They didn't see anyone else as a leader other than Aparajit for most of their lifetime. You didn't get an opportunity yet to prove that you can lead them. Maybe the announcement is the first step for them to appreciate your plan of consolidating and rebuilding.' Chitraangad tried to cheer up his friend.

'True,' Mitrajit nodded at his friend's statement as he took the palm leaf with the announcement and put the seal of Devasthana on it before giving it to Arochan.

---

[98] Flying plane/vehicle

'There is one thing that I am not clear about, though,' Arochan said. 'As I was checking with everyone in the village, Viraata's wife inquired about him. It looks like he didn't come back to Devasthana after leaving the war camp. She is very concerned now and is planning to leave with her kids immediately to her parental home.'

'Oh yes, totally forgot about that coward.' Chitraangad replied. 'Hope he didn't get into any trouble on the way back. He definitely was not in the right state of mind.'

Mitrajit responded, 'That's interesting. I hope he is safe and will come here soon. Anyways, let us get on with our plans. If he is safe and hopefully joins us, then we will have more support here at Devasthana. I will tell Dhruti to check on his wife and provide some comfort to her.'

******

'I feel bad about going to another village and giving them the same bad news,' Arochan told Aayusha just as they left the fourth village on their journey. 'Just look at how everyone is reacting. Do you think they will join the rest of us at Devasthana? I highly doubt it.'

Aayusha looked at Arochan and could sense the pain and worry the young man was going through. He himself had experienced the pain and challenges of losing family and migrating to other places to settle down. It was one thing to hear the bad news, but also challenging to be the bearer of it.

'I understand your concerns Arochan. It is not easy, and I agree with you, but right now all we can do is convey the plans. For now, let us continue and hopefully get back to Devasthana sooner.'

As they moved on to the next village, they stopped at a small stream to refill their water bags and give their tired legs and minds some rest.

As he sat down on a small rock beside the stream, Arochan's eyes spotted a dark figure in between the trees just to his right. He jolted at the sight of a person rushing towards him with a sword. The person's face was hidden behind the cloth of his turban but could still see the tripundra[99] on his forehead.

Just as Arochan was about to shout and give a warning to Aayusha, he saw that Aayusha was quick enough and pushed the attacker aside while slicing the attacker's arm with his sword. Just then, two other attackers came out of the bushes from Arochan's left side. He immediately rushed towards them and stopped one of their blows with his shield while blocking the others with his sword. He pushed both with a strong force and started to counterattack them.

Within seconds, both Arochan and Aayusha were surrounded by seven of the attackers, but they were able tackle all of them. The attackers were unable to withstand the counterattack from the two young men. Within minutes, they had six of them dead.

[99] Three lines drawn with Ash – worn by Lord Shiva's followers

Aayusha whistled and pointed to the one attacker who was still breathing. The attacker was wounded but still alive. Arochan was about to run towards the attacker and stab him with his sword when Aayusha stopped him with his own sword.

'It is better to know who these attackers were,' Aayusha said.

'It is clear from their peculiar tripundra on their forehead. These dastard attackers are Ekapaadas,' Arochan replied, still seething with anger.

Aayusha now understood why Arochan was intending to kill the attacker. Moving Arochan slowly to the side, he bent forwards and asked the lone Ekapaada. 'What is your name? What are your intentions? How many are you?'

The injured Ekapaada looked at him and said 'Please give me some water. My name is Neelakanta. I will tell you everything. Please don't kill me.'

Aayusha looked at Arochan and signed him to give some water to Neelakanta. Arochan hesitatingly handed his bag of water to Aayusha.

Aayusha propped up Neelakanta's head and gave him some water. 'Now tell me, Neelakanta. What are you all doing around here? I don't want to hurt you, but if you don't answer the truth, my friend here is eager to kill you,' he said.

Neelakanta nodded slowly and gasped for breath. 'We were sent by our leader, Mahendra, to scout the nearby villages. We got news that the most of the Kalingas got killed in the war and that there are very few left in their kingdom. Mahendra felt that they are not in any position to support you and wanted to get a gauge on how many of you are left. He is planning for a full attack on the Devasthana. There is another group of scouts going around the eastern side of the region. They may have already reached back to Bhadrakaleswar, to inform our leader.'

'So, what did you see then? What message were you planning to take back to your cunning leader?' Arochan was furious at the news of Ekapaadas planning to attack them at their most vulnerable period.

Aayusha looked at Arochan and signed with his hand to cool down. He looked at Neelakanta and asked, 'What were you planning to inform them of? If you were here for scouting purposes, then why did you attack us?'

Neelakanta took a deep breath. 'We saw that most of the villagers were packing up. We also heard families talking about how most of you were killed in the war and not many of you were left. We were returning back to our capital when we saw both of you sitting at the stream. Our captain told us to attack you as he planned to take you both to our leader to have you as a ransom in case we needed to.' Neelakanta looked down with guilt as he said that.

'How low of your kind to plan to attack us in these times of distress!' Arochan spat. 'What do you want to loot from these villagers who have lost everything?' he said furiously at Neelakanta.

'I understand your pain,' Neelakanta replied while not making an eye contact with Arochan. 'I was just following what our leader told us and my captain told me.' He said while pointing to one of the dead attackers nearby. 'Please spare me. If you leave me, I can go and warn them not to attack. I have kids at home. Please leave me.' Neelakanta pleaded with them with hope that his revealing the secrets would help him to be spared.

'In your dreams. You said your other group must have already gone and informed your leader,' Arochan said. 'We should immediately go to Devasthana and let Mitrajit and pitashri know about this,' he said, looking at Aayusha.

Aayusha pulled Arochan to the side and whispered, 'I have an idea. Let me take him along with me to Devasthana and convey the plans of attack by Ekapaadas. You better go and communicate with other villages to let them know about Mitrajit's plans and also about the plans of Ekapaadas. May be this will convince majority of them to come to Devasthana. We don't have much time.'

'Good idea. But let us kill this low Ekapaada here. There is no need to take him to the Devasthana. What use will he be?' Arochan was not convinced of Aayusha taking Neelakanta.

'Well, we can squeeze out as much information from him if we keep him alive. We can try to get more insight into their plans. If it doesn't work out, then you can put him down, but for now let us do this,' Aayusha replied.

Arochan nodded hesitantly. 'Okay. Be careful as we don't know who else is around and scouting. Tell them to review the defenses. I will try to get as many villagers as possible so that we can put up some fight. Tell Mitrajit to send a message to Kalinga. Maybe General Pattabhadra will be able to send some help soon.'

*****

Mitrajit tried to convince Kumudini one last time to stay as she put her bags in the bullock cart. 'It will be a morale booster for the rest of the tribe to see their leader Aparajit's legacy continue even when he is not alive,' he said to Kumudini.

Kumudini didn't seem convinced to stay. 'I understand your plans, Mitra, and whole heartedly agree. Even Aparajit would have done the same. But I cannot stay in this village without him. His memories will haunt me forever. What do you think Dhruti or Subhadra would have done if they were in my situation? It is not easy for us. But I leave with the trust that whoever is planning to stay back in Devasthana are going to be in good hands with you and Chitraangad leading them.'

Both Mitrajit and Chitraangad bent down to touch her feet.

'Bless you both. May you both be successful in your plans,' Kumudini said and went to sit in the cart. The bullock cart slowly started moving ahead with dozens of other carts following her out of Devasthana. Shanthan and Chandra both accompanied the convoy of the carts until the outskirts of Devasthana.

Both Dhruti and Subhadra couldn't hold back their tears as they bid adieu to Kumudini who was like mentor for them for all these years.

'What impact just two days of participating in that war has had on us Ustrakarnikas; imagine what must be happening around the

Bharata varsha now. I hope we can get some updates soon from someone from the warfront,' said Mitrajit.

Chitraangad replied, 'I can't wait to hear the outcome too. Hope the war has ended by now. I hope the Kuru family has gotten the result they wanted. History may remember either the Pandavas or the Kauravas and the many royals who fought in this war, but no one will remember the thousands of normal soldiers who gave up their lives in this war. I hope that historians one day will also highlight about the various tribes who have participated in this war.'

'True, Chitra. It makes me think that we should have an inscription on the stones here at the chatvaram with a list of our fallen fellow Ustrakarnikas. I hope that the future generations will appreciate our participation in the Kurukshetra war and the sacrifices our people made.'

Maarthanda replied, 'Great idea, Mitra. I will have Shiva and Mareechi help me with the inscriptions.'

'Well, there is no one else left than us few to do this now.' Chitraangad replied with a low sigh. 'I don't know what news Arochan is going to get back with.'

That afternoon, as Mitrajit was coming back from the chatvaram, he saw Purna sitting in front of the house all alone. She was devastated with her friend Bhumi's mother deciding to leave the village. Mitrajit bent towards Purna and said, 'I know you are sad about Bhumi leaving Devasthana.'

Purna looked at her father and tears rolled down her eyes. 'I am going to miss her, pitashri. Poor girl, she lost her father. She was supposed to be getting married soon. But now their family is shattered,' she said. 'What are we going to do?' she asked, still looking at her father. 'Are we also going to leave? Who am I going to play and study with if everyone starts leaving?'

Mitrajit was taken aback by her words. All this time, he was thinking of what may be good for the villagers and tried his best to keep all of them at Devasthana but never thought how his daughter was taking it in with her best friends leaving.

'I am so sorry about all that is happening, dear. I wish I had a better solution. But you know what? Even after they leave, you can always think of the nice memories you had with her. Why don't you go to her house and make the most of your time with her today before they leave tomorrow? I will tell amma.'

Purna looked at him and hugged him. 'Thanks, pitashri,' she said as she wiped her tears. 'I better be with her and recall our times together and let her leave with good memories.'

Purna ran towards the street as she said. Mitrajit's gaze followed her till she reached the turn at the end of the street. *Thank you, Lord Shiva, for blessing me with such a beautiful soul and bringing me back safely to her,* he thought.

He went inside the house but couldn't find Dhruti home. He went to the backyard and was surprised to see Dhruti sitting alone with her forehead resting on her knees. 'What happened, dear? Why are you sitting here alone?' he asked.

'Oh, you are here. Sorry,' she said while wiping her tears away. 'I was feeling a bit low. Most of the villagers left, some of whom I have grown older with. So many friends I have made over these years. Even Kumudini left. How can I be happy when people around me have lost so many of their loved ones?'

Mitrajit took a deep breath. Dhruti was right. He was happy to see her and Purna again, but at the same time couldn't express that happiness when so many had been impacted by this war. He sat down beside her. Holding her hand, he said, 'All we can wish now is for better times, Dhruti. I wish the outcome could have been different. I wish there had not been a war in the first place. This war could have been avoided if Duryodhana would have agreed to give the five villages to Pandavas when asked, and we would not have seen this day.'

Both sat down there for some time, looking at the Peepal tree in their backyard while lost in their own thoughts. How their lives had changed in the span of a month!

*****

'This was something we were expecting, but I didn't think they were planning to attack so soon,' Mitrajit whispered to Chitraangad when Aayusha brought forward Neelakanta and informed them about the Ekapaadas scouts and probable next steps.

'Well, I think we need to act quickly. No matter how many may join us from other villages, I don't know how long we can hold them back. Anyways, let us first deal with this Ekapaada,' Chitraangad suggested to his friend.

'Now, you are going to tell me every plan your leader was making and how soon your leader was planning to attack Devasthana and other villages,' Mitrajit told Neelakanta with a stern voice. Chitraangad looked at his friend with a sense of appreciation as he could see Mitrajit was showing confidence as a leader.

'I don't know much, and you can believe me. I am just a soldier who has been put onto this scouting duty by my captain. We were told that the Kalingas lost a vast majority of their army in the Kurukshetra war, and so had yours. We were supposed to scout the villages and Devasthana to get a gauge on the current situation and report back. If the news of you all losing a vast number of men was found true from our scouting, then the plans were to attack Devasthana,' Neelakanta looked down to the ground as he spoke the last sentence.

'How soon were you planning to attack?' Mitrajit probed further still with a stern voice.

'It could be anytime, probably within the next day or two. The other group must have reached by this time, and they may already be on their way. Please let me go. I won't tell them that I met you. I will tell them that a group of bandits attacked my fellow scouts and killed them. I have kids at home to take care of. Please let me go,' Neelakanta tried his best to bow in front of Mitrajit though his wounds didn't allow him any further.

'Maarthanda, take him to our prison and tie him up there. We will think of what to do with this man later. We have other things to plan now,' Mitrajit announced.

'Please don't take me over to the prison. I promise, I told you everything. Please let me go to my kids,' Neelakanta continued to plead as Maarthanda took him towards prison.

'This prison has been empty, for some years, but thanks to you, it will be filled up again,' Maarthanda said along the way.

Mitrajit looked at Aayusha and said, 'Thank you very much. You can imagine what dangers we have been facing and the reason for us to be attached with this war.' Looking at Chitraangad, Mitrajit continued, 'I have doubts now on our plan to have everyone come here and rebuild Chitra. With so few of us capable of defending I am a bit worried how well we can defend everyone from the Ekapaadas. What if we cannot keep our people safe? Maybe it was better for them to go wherever they were planning to.'

'Now, don't get discouraged my friend. Let us wait for Arochan to come. He should be here anytime. Let's see what the status is from across the villages. Meanwhile, we should look at reviewing our defenses. Let's put everyone who is left on alert,' Chitraangad suggested.

'Absolutely. Let us review our defenses and inform everyone who has stayed back to be on alert. Aayusha, please take rest and once Arochan arrives, you can review the Eastern side defenses along with him. Meanwhile, please have Sharath join Mareechi and Shiva and review the defenses on the Southern side. I will get Maarthanda to join Chandra to check on the North side. I will review the West end,' Mitrajit said while slowly turning towards Chitraangad. He continued 'with Chitra.'

Chitraangad gave an acknowledging smile to his friend.

'Sure thing,' Aayusha replied and went on to speak to Sharath and Chandra. The three of them looked fit, tough and very active. *No surprise as to why the Narayani sena are so well respected,* Mitrajit thought.

'Thanks for including me with you, Mitra,' Chitraangad said.

'Of course, my friend. You are still capable of sending shivers into enemy ranks. How are you feeling, by the way?'

'I am much better. Subhadra has been feeding me nutritious food and fruits. You can see the stump is also healing well,' Chitraangad pointed to his cut arm as he said that.

'Good to know, Chitra. Now let's see what information Arochan gets back with. Also, I am still uncertain.' Mitrajit paused for a moment before continuing, 'Maybe we should think of alternate plans now that we know that Ekapaadas have planned to attach us soon.'

'Well, you are right. Maybe we should send a message to Kalingas. I know it's been only few days that they left to their home, but just having the Kalingas on our side could make Ekapaadas think twice,' Chitraangad replied.

'Yes, and maybe we can see how we can use Neelakanta to send that message to the Ekapaada leader. Hopefully that can buy us some time,' Mitrajit said.

'Great minds think alike,' Chitraangad replied. 'I was also thinking in the same lines. Let's discuss that option in the evening once we hear from Arochan. Meanwhile, let me talk to Mareechi. He can go to Kalinga kingdom as our messenger.'

'Sure. Makes sense,' Mitrajit replied.

By evening, it was communicated to others in Devasthana to stay alert. Arochan arrived with the news that some families were interested and that up to a hundred may join by the next day at Devasthana, while a majority of the families still decided to leave.

'The news that Ekapaadas were scouting didn't help,' Arochan said. 'I thought that may prompt many to come to Devasthana, but most of them felt it was good for them to not join us to avoid the Ekapaadas.'

'Well, there is nothing else we can do. All we need to do is review our defenses for now. Mareechi agreed to leave tomorrow morning to Kalinga kingdom.,' Chitraangad replied while explaining the plan to Arochan and Aayusha.

'If you all can excuse me, there is something that I have been thinking of telling you. I have a suggestion,' Aayusha asked.

Mitrajit looked at him curiously. 'What is it, Aayusha?'

'I was thinking that since there are just a hundred of the Ustrakarnikas left, maybe you can try what our prince Krishna has done with the Yadavas. I know we all can try our best to defend against the Ekapaadas. But is it worth it to lose any more lives in that battle? We don't know how many of them will attack Devasthana. I thought it may be wise to leave Devasthana and go somewhere far away with the group. Maybe go towards Kalinga or maybe even to

Dwarka.' Aayusha took a pause to check the reactions to his suggestion. Everyone around seemed surprised.

'Kalingas may support you, but they themselves are weakened,' Aayusha continued. 'And we don't know the outcome of the war as and which other allies may come to Kalinga's support. But one thing is for sure, the Yadavas will not be affected as we still have most of our army and Balarama is still at Dwarka as he was not fighting the Kurukshetra war. I know the Yadavas will welcome you with wide open arms.'

Mitrajit took a moment to process the suggestion. He looked around to see what others were thinking. Everyone was taking time to think.

'That is something I have not thought of, Aayusha, but thanks for suggesting,' Mitrajit broke the silence.

'What are Ustrakarnikas without Devasthana?' Chitraangad jumped in.

'I agree, Chitraangad,' Aayusha replied. 'But who are Ustrakarnikas if none of you are left here. We are still Yadavas because of our people, our culture and heritage and didn't lose that even after moving from Mathura.'

Chitraangad stopped for a second and nodded slowly as he couldn't argue with that statement made by Aayusha. The young man's argument made sense. *Who are Ustrakarnikas without their people?* he thought.

Mitrajit listened to Aayusha's point and said, 'I mean, it is definitely an interesting proposition, Aayusha,' he continued. 'Our people need to be in a safe situation whether it's at Devasthana or anywhere else. Maybe we can wait to see if Kalingas may come to help us or not and then decide to move away from Devasthana.'

'But you make a good point too,' he continued. 'They themselves may still be reeling from their losses and may not be in a position to help us. But I never would have thought about moving to a place like Dwarka. Why would they allow us? Everyone else must already be at Dwarka's door asking for help. The idea is tempting, but I don't know if that is something your royalty will approve.' Mitrajit looked at Chitraangad again to see if he had any feedback.

'It is definitely a logical proposition, Aayusha,' Chitraangad said. 'I feel it is worth considering the move to Dwarka, but only if we are confident that the Yadavas will accept us.'

Aayusha was excited that his proposal was being considered. He immediately replied, 'I am very much confident that you will be well received. You can settle down around the mainland closer to Dwarka or even on the islands if they are comfortable with that. If you are still considering my proposal, I would suggest that we get going sooner rather than later.'

Mitrajit nodded and replied, 'As I think further, I am getting more convinced to move away from Devasthana at this point, but let us give ourselves tonight to think over this option. We will also have others join us by tomorrow and then we can decide. Meanwhile, we must make sure our defenses are good, and we need to be alert over the next few days. We never know when and how soon the

Ekapaadas may be looking to attack. Glad that these thugs didn't attack when we were in Kurukshetra. Now let us get going.'

'What do you say, Chitra?' Mitrajit asked his friend as they walked to check the western side fences.

'That young man made me think that it would be a wise decision to move away from Devasthana. We don't want to lose anyone further. We may be confident in our defenses, but we were also confident of winning in the war. I think we can keep the Ekapaadas at bay for a short time, but not forever. We also don't know how big the attack they are planning this time is, especially with the intelligence report they have of our numbers. We have a whole generation to take care of if we want Ustrakarnikas to survive into many more thousands of years. Let us hear from everyone else tomorrow and since most of those arriving will already be packed up, we could easily move out of Devasthana by the next day if needed,' Chitraangad replied.

'Well, that's a good point. I just want to hope that the Yadavas are as welcoming as Aayusha has been telling us.'

'That is something we have to trust with our instincts. He definitely seems confident. I mean, it was them who sent us him and the other two men to support us. They have good intentions.'

'Yes, Chitra. Let's hope for the best. It may be better if we also let the rest of the villagers here to be aware of our plans so that they're also packed up and be ready if everyone favors to move. Don't know what Dhruti and Subhadra will feel about this plan to move.'

'The only way to find out is to ask them.' Chitraangad replied.

After reviewing the defenses, Mitrajit and Chitraangad went to update Dhruti and Subhadra. They both were surprised with the idea of moving but at the same time supported the idea since they were worried about the Ekapaadas' plan to attack.

Leaving both of them to process the idea, Mitrajit and Chitraangad went around Devasthana to communicate the plans with the few families left. Whoever stayed back in Devasthana seemed interested in the idea.

Mitrajit called up Shiva and Mareechi and asked them to inscribe the names of the fallen soldiers on bronze plates along with on the stones. 'It will be easier to take the bronze plates with us if we leave and the stones can still be a reminder for anyone who visits the Devasthana region in the future,' he said.

Three more families arrived from Ramapura to settle down at Devasthana before the end of the night. Accommodations were provided to them. Dhruti and Subhadra checked in with them regularly to provide any necessary items.

In the night, as Mitrajit and Dhruti were packing, Purna came to them and said, 'Thanks for letting me spend my time with Bhumi. We talked a lot about the good memories we made. I felt good about that.'

Mitrajit smiled and replied, 'I'm glad, dear. Memories are what we all will take with us.'

'One more thing, pitashri,' she continued. 'I also wanted to appreciate your idea of inscribing names of the men who lost their lives in the war. Not everyone does that. I recall asking acharya ji as to why there were no inscriptions or names mentioned anywhere about the fallen *vanara*[100] who gave up their lives in the fight against Ravana.'

Mitrajit was amazed by her thoughts. Yes, he had only heard about Angad, Hanuman, Vali, and Sugriva and a few other vanara who fought alongside Ram against Ravana. But he had never come across the names of the other thousands of vanara who sacrificed their lives in that war. He was happy to see that his daughter appreciated his ideas.

Before they slept, Mitrajit confirmed once more with Dhruti. 'I hope you are comfortable with my plan, dear.'

'Of course, swami. I was talking to Subhadra too. We felt that it is a much better idea to move than always live here, fearing the Ekapaadas. We know that you all can thwart their attacks, but this is not how we talked about getting older. We want to enjoy the rest of our lives, get Purna married and look forward to spending time with our grand kids,' Dhruti replied.

'I know it is going to be hard for all of us to leave our house, the place where we grew up most of our lives,' she continued, 'but I think this is going to be best for us. Glad that the young Yadava suggested this.'

'Happy to hear that you are fine with the decision, dear,' Mitrajit said as he hugged Dhruti.

---

[100] Army of monkey tribe

*****

The next morning, as Mitrajit and Purna were tying up the cows to their bullock carts, they saw Arochan running towards them. 'Come to the chatvaram quickly. Viraata is here and he has Neelakanta with him,' he announced.

Mitrajit looked at Purna and said, 'Go and tell Amma that I am going to the chatvaram. Tell her to continue packing the kitchen items. I will be back soon.'

'What happened?' Mitrajit asked Arochan as they both rushed towards the village center.

'I don't know exactly, but it seems like Neelakanta tried to escape and Viraata found him at the outskirts of Devasthana. Looks like Viraata has been hesitating to come into Devasthana earlier, but I'm glad he found that Ekapaada thug and took him on,' Arochan replied.

As soon they arrived at chatvaram, Mitrajit looked around to see Neelakanta kneeling on the ground. Viraata was standing beside along with his wife and son.

Mitrajit looked towards Viraata expressing surprise at seeing him.

'After I left the war camp, all along the way to Devasthana I was thinking what everyone would think of me,' Viraata said. 'I felt that everyone would see me as someone who ran away from the war. With that guilt, I didn't dare to enter the Devasthana. I was just camping on the outskirts of the village at the southern end. Then, a few days ago I saw Arochan with another person passing by and overheard them talking about the losses we had to incur in the war. I wanted to come immediately but was still hesitant. My thought was to meet my family and leave with them to my wife's parental village and settle down there.' Viraata looked at the ground with a guilty feeling as he said that.

'Earlier today, I heard some rustling in the woods and saw this man running away. It didn't feel normal. I encountered him and saw the tripundra and identified him as an Ekapaada. I stopped and tied him up. After questioning, he mentioned what happened with him. I am sorry for leaving you all at the war and running away from my responsibilities. But I am one of you. One of the Ustrakarnikas and I should be with you. Whatever decision you make, I will stand by it. I promise that on my son's life.'

Mitrajit looked at Viraata. He went closer to him and hugged him. 'Nice to see you, Viraata. We all make mistakes, but I am glad that you are with us now. I feel much supported. Every one of us is needed to fight back the Ekapaadas until we plan our next steps,' he said.

Looking down towards Neelakanta, Mitrajit addressed him, 'You should have been grateful to us for not taking your life. You have shown your true colors, Ekapaada. But don't worry. We don't kill our prisoners and stoop to your level. We have decided to leave Devasthana and settle in a distant place. Now go and tell your leader to leave us alone. Tell him to spare his men's lives too. If he still attacks us, then every Ustrakarnika, whether it's a man or woman or a kid, will ensure we will fight our best and kill as many Ekapaadas as we can. But we don't want any more bloodbath. We all have already lost much. With us gone, your tribe will have access to the resources of this region. Be happy and be thankful that your tribe has survived, unlike us. Now leave this place before I change my decision.'

Everyone looked at Mitrajit in surprise. Chitraangad came closer to his friend and whispered, 'Are you sure, Mitra? Leaving him may not be a good idea.'

Mitrajit looked at Chitraangad and said, 'Whether we leave him or not, we know that the Ekapaadas are going to attack us anyways. At least through this person, we can send a message that we don't want any more fights and that we are leaving this place. Hopefully, that will make them hold off their attack.'

Chitraangad nodded slowly in agreement. No matter what, Ekapaadas would attack. *It is better to use our resources to pack up quickly and leave than to think of how to handle them*, he thought.

Neelakanta looked up to Mitrajit and with folded hands said, 'Ustrakarnika. Salute. You have proven to be a wise leader with good heart. Thank you for sparing my life. I will go back and inform your decision to my leader. I hope that he will give a thought to not attacking you. Me and my family will be forever grateful for your gesture. Thank you and I wish you all a safe move.'

Neelakanta bowed to everyone and slowly started his journey back.

More families from the other Ustrakarnika villages arrived before noon. Mitrajit informed everyone who arrived of his plans. 'You are

259

welcome to go wherever you want to if you are not interested in coming with us,' he said.

One of the elders came forward and said, 'There is a reason why we wanted to join you here at Devasthana. It is very important for us Ustrakarnikas to stand together in this hour of crisis, no matter how few of us are left. Your plan to move to a safer place, that too to a place like Dwarka, is much appreciated too. That way we will also be safe from the continuous attacks from Ekapaadas. It totally makes sense.'

'It is not the place where we live that makes us Ustrakarnikas, but it is our culture that makes us who we are. We can continue our practices, teach our kids about our culture, and they can continue to be Ustrakarnikas in the future,' acharya ji said, endorsing Mitrajit's plan.

'Now that everyone who is left supports your plan, I think we have enough endorsement to move to Dwarka and we need to move out quickly,' Chitraangad said to Mitrajit. Maarthanda and Viraata nodded in agreement.

Mitrajit looked at Aayusha one more time to get the reassurance that the Yadavas would welcome them. Aayusha nodded.

'Everyone, listen,' Mitrajit said as he stood on the platform near the chatvaram. 'The decision to participate in the Kuru family war was with the intention to keep everyone safe from the Ekapaadas in the future. Though we had losses, our intention is still to keep the rest of us safe from them. After talking to you all and thinking about it, I have made the decision that we will all move tomorrow morning at first light towards Dwarka. Our friend, Aayusha has assured us that the Yadavas will welcome us to settle down with them and I know if that happens, we will be much safer there than here. You all are welcome to leave if you do not agree with this decision. We will respect that too. But for now, whoever is ready to move, let us start gathering our things, get our carts ready and move on towards Dwarka.'

The few hundred who were left in Devasthana looked content with the decision. Most of them had already lost men in their families and felt at least this decision would help to save their future generations. The thought that they had a chance to live in a place ruled by Krishna and Balarama gave them the confidence of safety.

*****

That evening, everyone looked busy getting ready for the trip. Mitrajit ensured that the patrol group was still active to ensure they would be alerted in case Ekapaadas attacked that night. One more night and hopefully the message from Neelakanta would persuade the Ekapaadas not to attack.

Before going to rest, Mitrajit went and sat alone in the backyard looking towards the Peepal tree. *So many memories,* he thought. He took a deep breath and sat in the meditation pose. Purna came and sat beside him to meditate. Mitrajit looked at her and gave a smile.

'I didn't know you started meditating too,' Mitrajit said looking at her.

'Yes, pitashri. I wanted to make sure we continued what grandmother had taught you.'

Mitrajit was amazed by her response. He looked at her and smiled. It was for these moments that he always craved for, and he felt good about the decision he had taken to move out of Devasthana. Now he could be confident of having many more moments with his daughter. They both slowly went into the meditative stage.

Mitrajit and others took turns that night to patrol around Devasthana.

Before going to rest for the night, Mitrajit connected with Aayusha and said, 'One thing we should be careful of are the bandits in the Dandakaranya forest. That spot is notorious for them.'

'I agree, we can space ourselves with the caravan so that we have some protection around. I, along with Shanthan and Chandra, can pace along the lines to ensure we are ready to support if the need comes. We can take the path that goes through Janasthana where the mighty Godavari river starts its flow; that way we can be just on the outskirts of the forest all along the way. That may help us to avoid them.'

'From there, we will go northwards towards the Narmada River,' Aayusha continued, 'before going west to reach the Gomati river. If we go along the Gomati River, we will reach Dwarka's mainland in the next four to five days if we factor in day breaks and night camps.'

'Thank you very much, Aayusha. I will see you again in the morning. Hope you can get some rest too.'

'See you tomorrow, Mitrajit. Good night.'

As the sun rose on the east, Chitraangad went around to check on the patrolling groups. There was still no sign of the Ekapaadas.

Slowly, everyone started coming towards the outskirts with their bullock carts filled with grains, vegetables, and necessary household goods.

'Do you know that you are going to Dwarka and Krishna loves being with cows. You may get a chance to see him,' Purna whispered to the cows, Tulasi and Gowri.

Dhruti and Subhadra ensured all the kids and women were all set for the move, especially the ones who moved into Devasthana the previous day.

'Thank you, Aayusha. We all will be ever grateful to you. Your idea is going to save a whole generation of Ustrakarnikas,' Chitraangad said as he came along with Subhadra and Arochan along with their cart.

'Oh, please don't say that. I am glad that you have taken my suggestion. I will go ahead and let Shanthan lead the way at the front, and myself and Chandra will be taking turns with him,' Aayusha replied.

Mitrajit ensured the stone inscriptions were put in place at the chatvaram. He loaded the bronze plates in his cart and went to join the others. Once everyone joined the group, Mitrajit signaled acharya to announce the journey.

Acharya ji came forward in front of the group and blew the conch to signal their journey's start. 'Lord Shiva, please keep us

Ustrakarnikas safe and bless us as we take this important journey,' he said as he looked up towards the sky. Everybody started moving west.

Most of them turned back to take a last peek at Devasthana before entering the woods. The place that had been home to Ustrakarnikas for generations now appeared lonely, deserted.

'Hope we can come back again to check on the village later,' Chitraangad said to Subhadra and Arochan as he gave one last glance towards Devasthana.

Seeing Mitrajit turn around to take a last look at Devasthana, Purna and Dhruti also looked towards their village.

'Well, we will make new memories at the new place, pitashri,' Purna said. Mitrajit and Dhruti looked at her and nodded.

With that, the three of them turned back towards the woods and started their journey to Dwarka.

End Note

Now that you have completed reading this book, I hope that you have enjoyed the experience. I will be ever grateful if you can please review the book on Amazon site and leave a rating. As a self-published author, it will help me in reaching out to a wider audience.

I look forward to you all reading the second book in this series that will be out soon - Janya Bharata: The Deluge.

Glossary of Terms

Aavrutti - Return or Returning

Acharya - Teacher

Akshauhini - A battle formation or unit consisting of 21,870 each of chariots and elephants, 65,160 horses and 109,350 of infantry

Amma - Mother/Mom

Angavastram - Cloth worn on torso

Aranyagaya - Hymns of forest

Astapada - Precursor to chess

Bhaisajya - Healing

Bharata varsha - Indian subcontinent/land

Bhils - A tribe in central and mid-western ancient India. Mostly hunters and fishermen

Bhitti - Woven mat

Braathaa - Brother

Brahma muhurta - Approximately 1.5hr before sunrise

Chatvaram - Four corners or Crossroads or main center of village

Dandakaranya - thick forest area in ancient central India

Devatas - Gods

Dhanurveda - Military skills

Dharma yuddha - Ethical war. War fought with righteousness

Dweep - Island

Ganitam - Mathematics

Garuda Vyuha - Strategy or formation in Eagle shape

Gaudi - Alcoholic drink fermented from jaggery

Ghadiya - Unit of Time: One ghadiya equals approximately 24 minutes

Gurukul - School

Howdah - A seat for riding on the back of an elephant or camel

Ishukruth - Preparation

Itihaasa - History

Jai - Hail

Ji - A mark of respect. Like Sir or Madam

Jyotirlinga - Special shrine where Lord Shiva is worshiped

Jyotishya - Astrology

Khadga vidya - Sword fighting

Kos - Unit of distance. Approximately 2 miles

Kshatriya - Warrior clan or background

Lakshagriham - palace made from wax

Linga - Idol for worshiping Lord Shiva

Maata - Mother

Maharathi, Athirathi, and Rathi - Different military ranks based on the warrior's capacity to fight

Mahout - Keeper of driver of an elephant

Moksha - Emancipation or liberation

Muhurat - Auspicious time of the day

Namaskaram - Felicitations or Greetings

Naraka - Hell

Padmasana - Crossed legged sitting

Paisti - Grain fermented alcoholic drink like beer

Palash - A tropical tree like teak

Paridhana - Lower garment or clothing

Parva - Episode/Chapter

Paschim saagara - Current Arabian Sea

Peepal - A species of fig tree

Pitashri - Father/Dad

Pooja - Prayer

Prabhu - Sir or Lord, mark of respect

Pranam - Salutation

Prauga chithi - Platform in shape of triangle

Pulasa - Ilis or Hilsa fish

Puranas - Historical scriptures

Purva - Before/Prior

Rajasuya Yagna - Imperial sacrifice or royal inauguration or consecration of king

Rangavalli - Rangoli. Patterns made from powdered limestone

Saagara - Ocean/Sea

Sahapankti bhojanam - Community lunch or get together

Samaveda - one of the vedic scriptures

Samudyama - Readiness

Sanhanan - Patience or Hardening of soul

Sanyasi - Renunciation

Sarvatomukhi Danda - Formation where best commanders will form a circle supported by flanks on either side

Sena - army

Sethu - Bridge

Shankhodara - In shape of a conch/shell

Shayana chithi - Platform in shape of Eagle/Falcon

Shivalinga - Lord Shiva's symbol

Smriti - Memories

Sri - Mark of respect like Sir

Swami - Husband or mark of respect

Taatsri - Uncle

Thathaastu - Blessing or outcomes

Tilakam - Mark made on forehead with vermillion or sandalwood

Tripundra - Three lines drawn with Ash - worn by Lord Shiva's followers

Urdhva Pundra - A pattern with a vertical line between a U-shaped marking

Uttarayan - Winter Solstice

Vaidya - Doctor or medic

Vaikuntam - God's abode

Vajra - Diamond

Vajraghaata - Shock/shocking outcomes

Vanabhojanam - Having lunch as a group under a tree or in a garden

Vanara - Army of monkey tribe

Vatsanikanth - Affection towards offspring

Vedas - Religious scriptures

Vimana - Flying plane or vehicle

Vyaghreswara - Another name for Lord Shiva

Yagna - Special prayer or ceremonial rights to God

Yava - Barley. Commonly used grain in ancient India around 6000BCE

Yojanas - A unit of distance. About 10 to 15 kilometers

Yuddha – War

Manufactured by Amazon.ca
Bolton, ON

29575626R00159